LITTLE TOWN
on the PRAIRIE

BY *Laura Ingalls Wilder*

ILLUSTRATED BY GARTH WILLIAMS

HarperTrophy®
An Imprint of HarperCollins*Publishers*

The LITTLE HOUSE BOOKS

by Laura Ingalls Wilder
Illustrated by Garth Williams

LITTLE HOUSE IN THE BIG WOODS

FARMER BOY

LITTLE HOUSE ON THE PRAIRIE

ON THE BANKS OF PLUM CREEK

BY THE SHORES OF SILVER LAKE

THE LONG WINTER

LITTLE TOWN ON THE PRAIRIE

THESE HAPPY GOLDEN YEARS

THE FIRST FOUR YEARS

CONTENTS

LITTLE TOWN
on the PRAIRIE

SURPRISE

One evening at supper, Pa asked, "How would you like to work in town, Laura?" Laura could not say a word. Neither could any of the others. They all sat as if they were frozen. Grace's blue eyes stared over the rim of her tin cup, Carrie's teeth stayed bitten into a slice of bread, and Mary's hand held her fork stopped in the air. Ma let tea go pouring from the teapot's spout into Pa's brimming cup. Just in time, she quickly set down the teapot.

"What did you say, Charles?" she asked.

"I asked Laura how she'd like to take a job in town," Pa replied.

"A job? For a girl? In town?" Ma said. "Why, what kind of a job—" Then quickly she said, "No, Charles,

1

I won't have Laura working out in a hotel among all kinds of strangers."

"Who said such a thing?" Pa demanded. "No girl of ours'll do that, not while I'm alive and kicking."

"Of course not," Ma apologized. "You took me so by surprise. What other kind of work can there be? and Laura not old enough to teach school yet."

All in the minute before Pa began to explain, Laura thought of the town, and of the homestead claim where they were all so busy and happy now in the springtime, and she did not want anything changed. She did not want to work in town.

SPRINGTIME
ON THE CLAIM

After the October Blizzard last fall, they had all moved to town and for a little while Laura had gone to school there. Then the storms had stopped school, and all through that long winter the blizzards had howled between the houses, shutting them off from each other so that day after day and night after night not a voice could be heard and not a light could be seen through the whirling snow.

All winter long, they had been crowded in the little kitchen, cold and hungry and working hard in the dark and the cold to twist enough hay to keep the fire going and to grind wheat in the coffee mill for the day's bread.

All that long, long winter, the only hope had been that sometime winter must end, sometime blizzards must stop, the sun would shine warm again and they could all get away from the town and go back to the homestead claim.

Now it was springtime. The Dakota prairie lay so warm and bright under the shining sun that it did not seem possible that it had ever been swept by the winds and snows of that hard winter. How wonderful it was, to be on the claim again! Laura wanted nothing more than just being outdoors. She felt she never could get enough sunshine soaked into her bones.

In the dawns when she went to the well at the edge of the slough to fetch the morning pail of fresh water, the sun was rising in a glory of colors. Meadow larks were flying, singing, up from the dew-wet grass. Jack rabbits hopped beside the path, their bright eyes watching and their long ears twitching as they daintily nibbled their breakfast of tender grass tips.

Laura was in the shanty only long enough to set down the water and snatch the milk pail. She ran out to the slope where Ellen, the cow, was cropping the sweet young grass. Quietly Ellen stood chewing her cud while Laura milked.

Warm and sweet, the scent of new milk came up from the streams hissing into the rising foam, and it mixed with the scents of springtime. Laura's bare feet were wet and cool in the dewy grass, the sunshine was warm on her neck, and Ellen's flank was warmer against her cheek. On its own little picket rope, Ellen's baby calf bawled anxiously, and Ellen answered with a soothing moo.

When Laura had stripped the last creamy drops of milk, she lugged the pail to the shanty. Ma poured some of the warm new milk into the calf's pail. The rest she strained through a clean white cloth into tin milk pans, and Laura carefully carried them down cellar while Ma skimmed thick cream from last night's milk. Then she poured the skimmed milk into the calf's pail, and Laura carried it to the hungry calf.

Teaching the calf to drink was not easy, but always interesting. The wobbly-legged baby calf had been born believing that it must butt hard with its little red poll, to get milk. So when it smelled the milk in the pail, it tried to butt the pail.

Laura must keep it from spilling the milk, if she could, and she had to teach it how to drink, because it didn't know. She dipped her fingers into the milk and let the calf's rough tongue suck them, and gently she led its nose down to the milk in the pail. The calf suddenly snorted milk into its nose, sneezed it out with a whoosh that splashed milk out of the pail, and then with all its might it butted into the milk. It butted so hard that Laura almost lost hold of the pail. A wave of milk went over the calf's head and a splash wet the front of Laura's dress.

So, patiently she began again, dipping her fingers for the calf to suck, trying to keep the milk in the pail and to teach the calf to drink it. In the end, some of the milk was inside the calf.

Then Laura pulled up the picket pins. One by one, she led Ellen, the baby calf and the yearling calf to fresh places in the soft, cool grass. She drove the iron pins deep into the ground. The sun was fully up now, the whole sky was blue, and the whole earth was waves of grass flowing in the wind. And Ma was calling.

"Hurry, Laura! Breakfast's waiting!"

In the shanty, Laura quickly washed her face and hands at the washbasin. She threw out the water in a sparkling curve falling on grass where the sun would swiftly dry it. She ran the comb through her hair, over her head to the dangling braid. There was never time before breakfast to undo the long braid, brush her hair properly, and plait it again. She would do that after the morning's work was done.

Sitting in her place beside Mary, she looked across the clean, red-checked tablecloth and the glinting dishes at little sister Carrie and baby sister Grace, with their soap-shining morning faces and bright eyes. She looked at Pa and Ma so cheerful and smiling. She felt the sweet morning wind from the wide-open door and window, and she gave a little sigh.

Pa looked at her. He knew how she felt. "I think, myself, it's pretty nice," he said.

"It's a beautiful morning," Ma agreed.

Then after breakfast Pa hitched up the horses, Sam and David, and drove them out on the prairie east of the shanty, where he was breaking ground for sod corn. Ma took charge of the day's work for the rest of them, and best of all Laura liked the days when she said, "I must work in the garden."

Mary eagerly offered to do all the housework, so that Laura could help Ma. Mary was blind. Even in the days before scarlet fever had taken the sight from her clear blue eyes, she had never liked to work outdoors in the sun and wind. Now she was happy to be useful indoors. Cheerfully she said, "I must work where I can see with my fingers. I couldn't tell the difference between a pea vine and a weed at the end of a hoe, but I can wash dishes and make beds and take care of Grace."

Carrie was proud, too, because although she was small she was ten years old and could help Mary do all the housework. So Ma and Laura went out to work in the garden.

People were coming from the East now, to settle all over the prairie. They were building new claim shanties to the east and to the south, and west beyond Big Slough. Every few days a wagon went by, driven by strangers going across the neck of the slough and northward to town, and coming back. Ma said there would be time to get acquainted when the spring work was done. There is no time for visiting in the spring.

Pa had a new plow, a breaking plow. It was wonderful for breaking the prairie sod. It had a sharp-edged wheel, called a rolling coulter, that ran rolling and cutting through the sod ahead of the plowshare. The sharp steel plowshare followed it, slicing underneath the matted grass roots, and the moldboard lifted the long, straight-edged strip of sod and turned it upside down. The strip of sod was exactly twelve inches wide, and as straight as if it had been cut by hand.

They were all so happy about that new plow. Now, after a whole day's work, Sam and David gaily lay down and rolled, and pricked their ears and looked about the prairie before they fell to cropping grass. They were not being worn down, sad and gaunt, by breaking sod that spring. And at supper, Pa was not too tired to joke.

"By jingo, that plow can handle the work by itself," he said. "With all these new inventions nowadays, there's no use for a man's muscle. One of these nights that plow'll take a notion to keep on going, and we'll look out in the morning and see that it's turned over an acre or two after the team and I quit for the night."

The strips of sod lay bottom-side-up over the furrows, with all the cut-off grass roots showing speckled in the earth. The fresh furrow was delightfully cool and soft to bare feet, and often Carrie and Grace followed behind the plow, playing. Laura would have liked to, but she was going on fifteen years old now, too old to play in the fresh, clean-smelling dirt. Besides, in the afternoons Mary must go for a walk to get some sunshine.

So when the morning's work was done, Laura took

Mary walking over the prairie. Spring flowers were blossoming and cloud-shadows were trailing over the grassy slopes.

It was odd that when they were little, Mary had been the older and often bossy, but now that they were older they seemed to be the same age. They liked the long walks together in the wind and sunshine, picking violets and buttercups and eating sheep sorrel. The sheep sorrel's lovely curled lavender blossoms, the clover-shaped leaves and thin stems had a tangy taste.

"Sheep sorrel tastes like springtime," Laura said.

"It really tastes a little like lemon flavoring, Laura," Mary gently corrected her. Before she ate sheep sorrel she always asked, "Did you look carefully? You're sure there isn't a bug on it?"

"There never are any bugs," Laura protested. "These prairies are so *clean!* There never was such a clean place."

"You look, just the same," said Mary. "I don't want to eat the only bug in the whole of Dakota Territory."

They laughed together. Mary was so light-hearted now that she often made such little jokes. Her face was so serene in her sunbonnet, her blue eyes were so clear and her voice so gay that she did not seem to be walking in darkness.

Mary had always been good. Sometimes she had been so good that Laura could hardly bear it. But now she seemed different. Once Laura asked her about it.

"You used to try all the time to be good," Laura said. "And you always were good. It made me so mad sometimes, I wanted to slap you. But now you are good without even trying."

Mary stopped still. "Oh, Laura, how awful! Do you ever want to slap me now?"

"No, never," Laura answered honestly.

"You honestly don't? You aren't just being gentle to me because I'm blind?"

"No! Really and honestly, no, Mary. I hardly think about your being blind. I—I'm just glad you're my sister. I wish I could be like you. But I guess I never can be," Laura sighed. "I don't know how you can be so good."

"I'm not really," Mary told her. "I do try, but if you could see how rebellious and mean I feel sometimes, if you could see what I really am, inside, you wouldn't want to be like me."

11

"I *can* see what you're like inside," Laura contradicted. "It shows all the time. You're always perfectly patient and never the least bit mean."

"I know why you wanted to slap me," Mary said. "It was because I was showing off. I wasn't really wanting to be good. I was showing off to myself, what a good little girl I was, and being vain and proud, and I deserved to be slapped for it."

Laura was shocked. Then suddenly she felt that she had known that, all the time. But, nevertheless, it was not true of Mary. She said, "Oh no, you're not like that, not really. You *are* good."

"We are all desperately wicked and inclined to evil as the sparks fly upwards," said Mary, using the Bible words. "But that doesn't matter."

"What!" cried Laura.

"I mean I don't believe we ought to think so much about ourselves, about whether we are bad or good," Mary explained.

"But, my goodness! How can anybody be good without thinking about it?" Laura demanded.

"I don't know, I guess we couldn't," Mary admitted. "I don't know how to say what I mean very well. But—it isn't so much thinking, as—as just knowing. Just being sure of the goodness of God."

Laura stood still, and so did Mary, because she dared not step without Laura's arm in hers guiding her. There Mary stood in the midst of the green and flowery miles of grass rippling in the wind, under the great blue sky and white clouds sailing, and she could not see. Everyone knows that God is good. But it seemed to Laura then that Mary must be sure of it in some special way.

"You are sure, aren't you?" Laura said.

"Yes, I am sure of it now all the time," Mary answered. "The Lord is my shepherd, I shall not want. He maketh me to lie down in green pastures, He leadeth me beside the still waters. I think that's the loveliest Psalm of all. Why are we stopping here? I don't smell the violets."

"We came by the buffalo wallow, talking," said Laura. "We'll go back that way."

When they turned back, Laura could see the low swell of land sloping up from the coarse grasses of Big Slough to the little claim shanty. It looked hardly larger than a hen coop, with its half-roof slanting up and stopping. The sod stable hardly showed in the wild grasses. Beyond them Ellen and the two calves were grazing, and to the east Pa was planting corn in the newly broken sod.

He had broken all the sod he had time to, before the ground grew too dry. He had harrowed the ground he had broken last year, and sowed it to oats. Now with a sack of seed corn fastened to a shoulder harness, and the hoe in his hand, he was going slowly across the sod field.

"Pa is planting the corn," Laura told Mary. "Let's go by that way. Here's the buffalo wallow now."

"I know," said Mary. They stood a moment, breathing in deeply the perfume of warm violets that came up as thick as honey. The buffalo wallow, perfectly round and set down into the prairie like a dish three or four feet deep, was solidly paved with violets. Thousands, millions, crowded so thickly that they hid their own leaves.

Mary sank down among them. "Mmmmmm!" she breathed. Her fingers delicately felt over the masses of petals, and down the thin stems to pick them.

When they passed by the sod field Pa breathed in a deep smell of the violets, too. "Had a nice walk, girls?" he smiled at them, but he did not stop working. He mellowed a spot of earth with the hoe, dug a tiny hollow in it, dropped four kernels of corn in the hollow, covered them with the hoe, pressed the spot firm with his boot, then stepped on to plant the next hill.

Carrie came hurrying to bury her nose in the violets. She was minding Grace, and Grace would play nowhere but in the field where Pa was. Angleworms fascinated Grace. Every time Pa struck the hoe into the ground she watched for one, and chuckled to see the thin, long worm make itself fat and short, pushing itself quickly into the earth again.

"Even when it's cut in two, both halves do that," she said. "Why, Pa?"

"They want to get into the ground, I guess," said Pa.

"Why, Pa?" Grace asked him.

"Oh, they just want to," said Pa.

"Why do they want to, Pa?"

"Why do you like to play in the dirt?" Pa asked her.

"Why, Pa?" Grace said. "How many corns do you drop, Pa?"

"Kernels," said Pa. "Four kernels. One, two, three, four."

"One, two, four," Grace said. "Why, Pa?"

"That's an easy one," said Pa.

> "One for the blackbird,
> One for the crow,
> And that will leave
> Just two to grow."

The garden was growing now. In tiny rows of different greens, the radishes, lettuce, onions, were up. The first crumpled leaves of peas were pushing upward. The young tomatoes stood on thin stems, spreading out their first lacy foliage.

"I've been looking at the garden, it needs hoeing," Ma said, while Laura set the violets in water to perfume the supper table. "And I do believe the beans will be up any day now, it's turned so warm."

All one hot morning, the beans were popping out of the ground. Grace discovered them and came shrieking with excitement to tell Ma. All that morning she could not be coaxed away from watching them. Up from the bare earth, bean after bean was popping, its stem uncoiling like a steel spring, and up in the sunshine the halves of the split bean still clutched two pale twin-leaves. Every time a bean popped up, Grace squealed again.

Now that the corn was planted, Pa built the missing half of the claim shanty. One morning he laid the floor joists. Then he made the frame, and Laura helped him raise it and hold it straight to the plumb line while he nailed it. He put in the studding, and the frames for two windows. Then he laid the rafters, to make the other slant of the roof that had not been there before.

Laura helped him all the time, Carrie and Grace watched, and picked up every nail that Pa dropped by mistake. Even Ma often spent minutes in idleness, looking on. It was exciting to see the shanty being made into a house.

When it was done, they had three rooms. The new part was two tiny bedrooms, each with a window. Now the beds would not be in the front room any more.

"Here's where we kill two birds with one stone," said Ma. "We'll combine spring housecleaning and moving."

They washed the window curtains and all the quilts and hung them out to dry. Then they washed the new

windows till they shone, and hung on them new curtains made of old sheets and beautifully hemmed with
Mary's tiny stitches. Ma and Laura set up the bedsteads in the new rooms all made of fresh, clean-
smelling boards. Laura and Carrie filled the straw
ticks with the brightest hay from the middle of a
haystack, and they made up the beds with sheets still
warm from Ma's ironing and with the clean quilts
smelling of the prairie air.

Then Ma and Laura scrubbed and scoured every
inch of the old shanty, that was now the front room. It
was spacious now, with no beds in it, only the cookstove and cupboards and table and chairs and the
whatnot. When it was perfectly clean, and everything
in place, they all stood and admired it.

"You needn't see it for me, Laura," Mary said. "I
can feel how large and fresh and pretty it is."

The fresh, starched white curtains moved softly in
the wind at the open window. The scrubbed board
walls and the floor were a soft yellow-gray. A bouquet
of grass flowers and windflowers that Carrie had
picked and put in the blue bowl on the table, seemed
to bring springtime in. In the corner the varnished
brown whatnot stood stylish and handsome.

The afternoon light made plain the gilded titles of
the books on the whatnot's lower shelf, and glittered
in the three glass boxes on the shelf above, each with
tiny flowers painted on it. Above them, on the next

shelf, the gilt flowers shone on the glass face of the clock and its brass pendulum glinted, swinging to and fro. Higher still, on the very top shelf, was Laura's white china jewel box with the wee gold cup and saucer on its lid, and beside it, watching over it, sat Carrie's brown and white china dog.

On the wall between the doors of the new bedrooms, Ma hung the wooden bracket that Pa had carved for her Christmas present, long ago in the Big Woods of Wisconsin. Every little flower and leaf, the small vine on the edge of the little shelf, and the larger vines climbing to the large star at the top, were still as perfect as when he had carved them with his jackknife. Older still, older than Laura could remember, Ma's china shepherdess stood pink and white and smiling on the shelf.

It was a beautiful room.

THE NECESSARY CAT

Now the first yellow-green spears of corn were dotted like fluttering ribbon-ends along the furrows of broken sod. One evening Pa walked across the field to look at them. He came back tired and exasperated.

"I've got to replant more than half the cornfield," he said.

"Oh, Pa. Why?" Laura asked.

"Gophers," said Pa. "Well, this is what a man gets for putting in the first corn in a new country."

Grace was hugging his legs. He picked her up and tickled her cheek with his beard to make her laugh. She remembered the planting rhyme, and sitting on his knee she chanted it proudly.

"One for the blackbird,
One for the crow,
And that will leave
Just two to grow."

"The man that made that up was an Easterner," Pa told her. "Out here in the Territory we'll have to make our own rhyme, Grace. How's this for a try?

"One for a gopher,
Two for a gopher,
Three for a gopher,
Four don't go fur."

"Oh, Charles," Ma protested, laughing. She did not think puns were funny, but she could not help laughing at the naughty look Pa gave her when he made one.

He had no sooner planted the seed corn than the striped gophers found it. All over the field they had been scampering, and stopping to dig into the little spots of fine soil with their tiny paws. It was a wonder that they knew exactly where the kernels were buried.

It was amazing that those little gophers, scampering, digging, sitting up straight and nibbling, each one, at one kernel of corn held in its paws, had eaten more than half of that whole field of corn.

"They are pests!" said Pa. "I wish we had a cat like old Black Susan used to be. She'd have thinned 'em out."

"I need a cat in the house, too," Ma agreed. "I declare the mice are getting so thick I can't leave food uncovered in the cupboard. Is there a cat to be had, Charles?"

"There's not a cat in this whole country, that I know of," Pa answered. "The storekeepers in town are complaining, too. Wilmarth's talking of getting a cat shipped out from the East."

That very night, Laura was startled out of a sound sleep. Through the partition between the bedrooms she heard a gasp, a grunt and a sudden thud of something small and squashing. She heard Ma say, "Charles! What is it?"

"I dreamed it," Pa said, low. "I dreamed a barber was cutting my hair."

Ma spoke low, too, because this was the middle of the night and the house was asleep. "It was only a dream. Lie down again and let me have some of the covers back."

"I heard the barber's shears go snip, snip," said Pa.

"Well, lie down and go to sleep," Ma yawned.

"My hair *was* being cut," said Pa.

"I never knew you to be upset by a dream before." Ma yawned again. "Lie down and turn over and you won't go on dreaming it."

"Caroline, my hair was being cut," Pa repeated.

"What do you mean?" Ma asked, more awake now.

"I am telling you," Pa said. "In my sleep I put up

21

my hand and— Here. Feel my head."

"*Charles!* Your hair's been *cut!*" Ma exclaimed. Laura heard her sit up in bed. "I can feel it, there's a place on your head—"

"Yes, that's the spot," said Pa. "I put up my hand—"

Ma interrupted. "A place as big as my hand, shorn clean off."

"I put up my hand," said Pa, "and I took hold of— something—"

"What? What was it?" Ma asked.

"I think," said Pa, "I think it was a mouse."

"*Where is it?*" Ma cried out.

"I don't know. I threw it away, as hard as I could," said Pa.

"My goodness!" Ma said weakly. "It must have been a mouse. Cutting off your hair to make itself a nest."

After a minute Pa said, "Caroline, I swear—"

"No, Charles," Ma murmured.

"Well, I would swear, if I did, that I can't lie awake nights to keep mice out of my hair."

"I do wish we had a cat," Ma wished hopelessly.

Sure enough, in the morning a mouse lay dead by the bedroom wall where Pa had thrown it. And Pa appeared at breakfast with an almost bare spot on the back of his head, where the mouse had shorn his hair away.

He would not have minded so much, but there was

not time for the hair to grow before he must go to a meeting of county commissioners. The country was settling so rapidly that already a county was being organized, and Pa must help. As the oldest settler, he could not shirk his duty.

The meeting was to be held at Whiting's homestead claim, four miles northeast of town. No doubt Mrs. Whiting would be there, and Pa could not keep his hat on.

"Never mind," Ma consoled him. "Just tell them how it happened. Likely they have mice."

"There'll be more important things to talk about," said Pa. "No, better just let them think this is the way my wife cuts my hair."

"Charles, you wouldn't!" Ma exclaimed, before she saw that he was teasing her.

When he drove away in the wagon that morning, he told Ma not to expect him for dinner. He had a ten-mile drive to make, on top of the time spent at the meeting.

It was supper time when he came driving to the stable. He unhitched and came hurrying to the house so quickly that he met Carrie and Grace running out.

"Girls! Caroline!" he called. "Guess what I've brought you!" His hand was in his pocket and his eyes were twinkling.

"Candy!" Carrie and Grace answered together.

"Better than that!" said Pa.

23

"A letter?" Ma asked.

"A paper," Mary guessed. "Maybe *The Advance*."

Laura was watching Pa's pocket. She was certain that something, not Pa's hand, was moving inside it.

"Let Mary see it first," Pa warned the others. He took his hand from his pocket. There on his palm lay a tiny blue and white kitten.

He laid it carefully in Mary's hand. She stroked its soft fur with a finger tip. Gently she touched its tiny ears and its nose and its wee paws.

"A kitten," she said wonderingly. "Such a very little kitten."

"Its eyes aren't open yet," Laura told her. "Its baby fur is as blue as tobacco smoke, and its face and its breast and its paws and the very tip of its tail are white. Its claws are the tiniest wee white things."

"It's too small to take from its mother," Pa said. "But I had to take it while I had the chance, before somebody else did. Whiting had the cat sent out to them from the East. She had five kittens, and they sold four of them today for fifty cents apiece."

"You didn't pay fifty cents for this kitten, Pa?" Laura asked him, wide-eyed.

"Yes, I did," said Pa.

Quickly Ma said, "I don't blame you, Charles. A cat in this house will be well worth it."

"Can we raise such a little kitten?" Mary asked anxiously.

"Oh, yes," Ma assured them. "We will have to feed it often, wash its eyes carefully, and keep it warm. Laura, find a small box and pick out the softest, warmest scraps from the scrap bag."

Laura made a snug, soft nest for the kitten in a pasteboard box, while Ma warmed some milk. They all watched while Ma took the kitten in her hand and fed it, a drop of milk at a time, from a teaspoon. The kitten's wee paws clutched at the spoon and its pink mouth tried to suck, and drop by drop it sucked in the warm milk, though some ran down its chin. Then they put it in its nest, and under Mary's warm hand it snuggled down to sleep.

"It has nine lives like any cat, and it will live all right," said Ma. "You'll see."

THE HAPPY DAYS

Pa said that the new town was growing fast. New settlers were crowding in, hurrying to put up buildings to shelter them. One evening Pa and Ma walked to town to help organize a church, and soon a foundation was laid for a church building. There were not carpenters enough to do all the building that was wanted, so Pa got carpenter work to do.

Every morning he did the chores and walked to town, taking a lunch in a tin pail. He began working promptly at seven o'clock, and by taking only a short nooning he was through work at half past six, and home again for a late supper. And every week he was earning fifteen dollars.

That was a happy time, for the garden was growing

well, the corn and oats were thriving, the calf was weaned so that now there was skim-milk for cottage cheese and there was cream to make butter and buttermilk, and best of all, Pa was earning so much money.

Often while Laura worked in the garden, she thought of Mary's going to college. It was nearly two years since they had heard there was a college for the blind in Iowa. Every day they had thought of that, and every night they prayed that Mary might go. The sorest grief in Mary's blindness was that it hindered her studying. She liked so much to read and learn, and she had always wanted to be a schoolteacher. Now she could never teach school. Laura did not want to, but now she must; she had to be able to teach school as soon as she grew old enough, to earn money for Mary's college education.

"Never mind," she thought, while she hoed, "I can see."

She saw the hoe, and the colors of the earth, and all the leafy little lights and shadows of the pea vines. She had only to glance up, and she saw miles of blowing grasses, the far blue skyline, the birds flying, Ellen and the calves on the green slope, and the different blues of the sky, the snowy piles of huge summer clouds. She had so much, and Mary saw only darkness.

She hoped, though she hardly dared to, that perhaps Mary might go to college that fall. Pa was making so much money. If Mary could only go now, Laura would study with all her might, she would work so hard that surely she could teach school as soon as she was sixteen years old, and then her earnings would keep Mary in college.

They all needed dresses and they all needed shoes, and Pa always had to buy flour and sugar and tea and salt meat. There was the lumber bill for the new half of the house, and coal must be bought for winter, and there were taxes. But this year there was the garden, and the corn and oats. By year after next, almost all they ate could be raised from the land.

If they had hens and a pig, they would even have meat. This was settled country now, hardly any game was left, and they must buy meat or raise it. Perhaps next year Pa could buy hens and a pig. Some settlers were bringing them in.

One evening Pa came home beaming.

"Guess what, Caroline and girls!" he sang out. "I saw Boast in town today, and he sent word from Mrs. Boast. *She's setting a hen for us!*"

"Oh, Charles!" Ma said.

"As soon as the chicks are big enough to scratch for themselves, he's going to bring us the whole batch," said Pa.

"Oh, Charles, this *is* good news. It's just like Mrs. Boast to do it, too," Ma said thankfully. "How is she, did he say?"

"Said they're getting along fine. She's so busy, she hasn't been able to get to town this spring, but she's certainly keeping you in mind."

"A whole setting of chicks," said Ma. "There's not many that would do it."

"They don't forget how you took them in when they came out here, just married, and got lost in a snowstorm, and we were the only settlers in forty miles," Pa reminded her. "Boast often speaks of it."

"Pshaw," said Ma. "That was nothing. But a whole setting of eggs— It saves us a year in starting a flock."

If they could raise the chicks, if hawks or weasels or foxes did not get them, some would be pullets that summer. Next year the pullets would begin laying, then there would be eggs to set. Year after next, there would be cockerels to fry, and more pullets to increase the flock. Then there would be eggs to eat, and when the hens grew too old to lay eggs, Ma could make them into chicken pie.

"And if next spring Pa can buy a young pig," said Mary, "then in a couple of years we'll have fried ham and eggs. And lard and sausages and spareribs and head-cheese!"

"And Grace can roast the pig's tail!" Carrie chimed in.

"Why?" Grace wanted to know. "What is a pig's tail?"

Carrie could remember butchering time, but Grace had never held a pig's skinned tail in front of the cookstove grate and watched it sizzling brown. She had never seen Ma take from the oven the dripping pan full of brown, crackling, juicy spareribs. She had never seen the blue platter heaped with fragrant sausage-cakes, nor spooned their red-brown gravy onto pancakes. She remembered only Dakota Territory, and the meat she knew was the salt, white, fat pork that Pa bought sometimes.

But someday they would have all the good things to eat again, for better times were coming. With so much work to do now, and everything to look forward to, the days were flying by. They were all so busy that they hardly missed Pa during the day. Then every night there was his coming home, when he brought news of the town, and they always had so much to tell him.

All day they had been saving a most exciting thing to tell him. They could hardly expect him to believe it, for this was what had happened:

While Ma was making the beds and Laura and Carrie were washing the breakfast dishes, they all heard the kitten cry out piteously. Kitty's eyes were open now and she could scamper across the floor, chasing a scrap of paper that Grace drew on a string.

"Grace, be careful!" Mary exclaimed. "Don't hurt the kitty."

"I'm not hurting the kitty," Grace answered earnestly.

Before Mary could speak, the kitten squalled again.

"Don't, Grace!" Ma said from the bedroom. "Did you step on it?"

"No, Ma," Grace answered. The kitten cried desperately, and Laura turned around from the dishpan.

"Stop it, Grace! What are you doing to the kitty?"

"I'm not doing anything to the kitty!" Grace wailed. "I can't find it!"

The kitten was nowhere to be seen. Carrie looked under the stove and behind the woodbox. Grace crawled under the tablecloth to see beneath the table. Ma looked under the whatnot's bottom shelf and Laura hunted through both bedrooms.

Then the kitten squalled again, and Ma found it behind the opened door. There, between the door and the wall, the tiny kitten was holding fast to a mouse. The mouse was full grown and strong, nearly as big as the wobbling little kitten, and it was fighting. It squirmed and bit. The kitten cried when the mouse bit her, but she would not let go. She braced her little legs and kept her teeth set in a mouthful of the mouse's loose skin. Her baby legs were so weak that she almost fell over. The mouse bit her again and again.

Ma quickly got the broom. "Pick up the kitten, Laura, I'll deal with the mouse."

Laura was obeying, of course, but she couldn't help saying, "Oh, I hate to, Ma! She's hanging on. It's her fight."

Right under Laura's grasping hand the tiny kitten made one great effort. She leaped onto the mouse. She held it down under both her front legs and screamed again as its teeth bit into her. Then her own little teeth snapped hard, into the mouse's neck. The mouse squeaked shrilly and went limp. All by herself, the kitten had killed it; her first mouse.

"I declare," Ma said. "Whoever heard of a cat-and-mouse *fight!*"

The baby kitten should have had its mother to lick its wounds and purr proudly over it. Ma carefully washed the bites and fed her warmed milk, Carrie and Grace stroked her wee nose and fuzzy soft head, and under Mary's warm hand she cuddled to sleep. Grace carried the dead mouse out by the tail and threw it far away. And all the rest of that day they often said, What a tale they had to tell Pa when he came home!

They waited until he had washed, and combed his hair, and sat down to supper. Laura answered his question about the chores; she had watered the horses and Ellen and the calves, and moved their picket pins. The nights were so pleasant now that she need not put them in the stable. They slept under the stars, and woke and grazed whenever they liked.

Then came the time to tell Pa what the kitten had done.

He said he had never heard anything like it. He looked at the little blue and white kitty, walking carefully across the floor with her thin tail standing straight up, and he said, "That kitten will be the best hunter in the county."

The day was ending in perfect satisfaction. They were all there together. All the work, except the supper dishes, was done until tomorrow. They were all enjoying good bread and butter, fried potatoes, cottage cheese, and lettuce leaves sprinkled with vinegar and sugar.

Beyond the open door and window the prairie was dusky but the sky was still pale, with the first stars beginning to quiver in it. The wind went by, and in the house the air stirred, pleasantly warmed by the cookstove and scented with prairie freshness and food and tea and a cleanness of soap and a faint lingering smell of the new boards that made the new bedrooms.

In all that satisfaction, perhaps the best part was knowing that tomorrow would be like today, the same and yet a little different from all other days, as this one had been. But Laura did not know this, until Pa asked her, "How would you like to work in town?"

WORKING IN TOWN

No one could imagine what work there could be for a girl in town, if it wasn't working as a hired girl in the hotel.

"It's a new idea of Clancy's," Pa said. Mr. Clancy was one of the new merchants. Pa was working on his store building. "We've got the store pretty near finished, and he's moving in his dry goods. His wife's mother's come West with them, and she's going to make shirts."

"Make shirts?" said Ma.

"Yes. So many men are baching on their claims around here that Clancy figures he'll get most of the trade in yard goods, with somebody there in the store making them up into shirts, for men that haven't got any womenfolks to do their sewing."

"That is a good idea," Ma had to admit.

"You bet! There's no flies on Clancy," said Pa. "He's got a machine to sew the shirts."

Ma was interested. "A sewing machine. Is it like that picture we saw in the *Inter-Ocean*? How does it work?"

"About like I figured out it would," Pa answered. "You work the pedal with your feet, and that turns the wheel and works the needle up and down. There's a little contraption underneath the needle that's wound full of thread, too. Clancy was showing some of us. It goes like greased lightning, and makes as neat a seam as you'd want to see.

"I wonder how much it costs," said Ma.

"'Way too much for ordinary folks," said Pa. "But Clancy looks on it as an investment; he'll get his money back in profits."

"Yes, of course," Ma said. Laura knew she was thinking how much work such a machine would save, but even if they could afford it, it would be foolish to buy one only for family sewing. "Does he expect Laura to learn how to run it?"

Laura was alarmed. She could not be responsible for some accident to such a costly machine.

"Oh, no, Mrs. White's going to run it," Pa replied. "She wants a good handy girl to help with the hand sewing."

He said to Laura: "She was asking me if I knew such a girl. I told her you're a good sewer, and she wants you to come in and help her. Clancy's got more orders for shirts than she can handle by herself. She says she'll pay a good willing worker twenty-five cents a day and dinner."

Quickly Laura multiplied in her head. That was a dollar and a half a week, a little more than six dollars a month. If she worked hard and pleased Mrs. White, maybe she could work all summer. She might earn fifteen dollars, maybe even twenty, to help send Mary to college.

She did not want to work in town, among strangers. But she couldn't refuse a chance to earn maybe fifteen dollars, or ten, or five. She swallowed, and asked, "May I go, Ma?"

Ma sighed. "I don't like it much, but it isn't as if you had to go alone. Your Pa will be there in town. Yes, if you want to, you may."

"I—don't want to leave you all the work to do," Laura faltered.

Carrie eagerly offered to help. She could make beds, and sweep, and do the dishes by herself, and weed in the garden. Ma said that Mary was a great help in the house, too, and now that the stock was picketed out, the evening's chores were not so much to do. She said, "We'll miss you, Laura, but we can manage."

There was no time to waste next morning. Laura brought the water and milked Ellen, she hurried to wash and to brush and braid her hair and pin it up. She put on her newest calico dress, and stockings and shoes. She rolled up her thimble in a freshly ironed apron.

The little breakfast that she had time to swallow had no taste. She tied on her sunbonnet and hurried away with Pa. They must be at work in town by seven o'clock.

Morning freshness was in the air. Meadow larks were singing, and up from Big Slough rose the thunder-pumps with long legs dangling and long necks out-stretched, giving their short, booming cry. It was a beautiful, lively morning, but Pa and Laura were too hurried. They were running a race with the sun.

Up rose the sun with no effort at all, while they kept walking as fast as they could, north on the prairie road toward the south end of Main Street.

The town was so changed that it seemed like a new place. Two whole blocks on the west side of Main Street were solidly filled with new, yellow-pine build-ings. A new board sidewalk was in front of them. Pa and Laura did not have time to cross the street to it. They hurried, Indian file, along the narrow dusty path on the other side of the street.

On this side, the prairie still covered all the vacant lots, right up to Pa's stable and his office-building at

38

the corner of Main and Second Streets. But beyond
them, on the other side of Second Street, the studding of a new building stood on the corner lot. Beyond
it, the path hurried past vacant lots again till it came
to Clancy's new store.

The inside of the store was all new, and still smelled

of pine shavings. It had, too, the faint starchy smell of bolts of new cloth. Behind two long counters, all along both walls ran long shelves, stacked to the ceiling with bolts of muslin and calicoes and lawns, challis and cashmeres and flannels and even silks.

There were no groceries, and no hardware, no shoes or tools. In the whole store there was nothing but dry goods. Laura had never before seen a store where nothing was sold but dry goods.

At her right hand was a short counter-top of glass, and inside it were cards of all kinds of buttons, and papers of needles and pins. On the counter beside it, a rack was full of spools of thread of every color. Those colored threads were beautiful in the light from the windows.

The sewing machine stood just behind the front end of the other counter, near that window. Its nickel parts and its long needle glittered and its varnished wood shone. A spool of white thread stood up on its thin black ridge. Laura would not have touched it for anything.

Mr. Clancy was unrolling bolts of calico before two customers, men in very dirty shirts. A large, fat woman with tight-combed black hair was pinning pattern pieces of newspaper to a length of checked calico spread on the counter near the sewing machine. Pa took off his hat and said good morning to her.

He said, "Mrs. White, here's my girl, Laura."

Mrs. White took the pins out of her mouth and said, "I hope you're a fast, neat sewer. Can you baste bias facings and make good firm buttonholes?"

"Yes, ma'am," Laura said.

"Well, you can hang your bonnet on that nail there, and I'll get you started," said Mrs. White.

Pa gave Laura a helping smile, and then he was gone.

Laura hoped that her trembly feeling would wear off, in time. She hung up her bonnet, tied on her apron, and put her finger into the thimble. Mrs. White handed her pieces of a shirt to baste together, and told her to take the chair in the window by the sewing machine.

Quickly Laura drew the straight-backed chair back a little way, so that the sewing machine partly hid her from the street. She bent her head over her work and basted rapidly.

Mrs. White did not say a word. Anxiously and nervously she kept fitting the pattern-pieces to the goods and cutting out shirt after shirt with long shears. As soon as Laura finished basting a shirt, Mrs. White took it from her and gave her another to baste.

After a time, she sat down at the machine. She whirled its wheel with her hand, and then her feet working fast on the pedal underneath kept the wheel whirring. The racketing hum of the machine filled Laura's head like the buzzing of a gigantic bumblebee.

The wheel was a blur and the needle was a streak of light. Mrs. White's plump hands scrambled on the cloth, feeding it rapidly under the needle.

Laura basted as fast as she could. She put the basted shirt on the shrinking pile at Mrs. White's left hand, seized pieces of the next one from the counter and basted it. Mrs. White took basted shirts from the pile, sewed them on the machine and piled them at her right hand.

There was a pattern in the way the shirts went, from the counter to Laura to a pile, from the pile to Mrs. White and through the machine to another pile. It was something like the circles that men and teams had made on the prairie, building the railroad. But only Laura's hands moved, driving the needle as fast as they could along the seams.

Her shoulders began to ache, and the back of her neck. Her chest was cramped and her legs felt tired and heavy. The loud machine buzzed in her head.

Suddenly the machine stopped, still. "There!" Mrs. White said. She had sewed the last basted shirt.

Laura had to gather a sleeve and to baste the armhole and the underarm seam. And the pieces of one more shirt lay waiting on the counter.

"I'll baste that one," Mrs. White said, snatching it up. "We're behindhand."

"Yes, ma'am," Laura said. She felt she should have worked faster, but she had done the best she could.

A big man looked in at the door. His dusty face was covered with an unshaved stubble of red beard. He called, "My shirts ready, Clancy?"

"Be ready right after noon," Mr. Clancy answered.

When the big man had gone on, Mr. Clancy asked Mrs. White when his shirts would be done. Mrs.

White said she did not know which shirts they were.
Then Mr. Clancy swore.

Laura scrooged small in her chair, basting as fast as
she could. Mr. Clancy snatched shirts from the pile
and almost threw them at Mrs. White. Still shouting
and swearing, he said she'd get them done before dinner or he'd know the reason why.

"I'll not be driven and hounded!" Mrs. White
blazed. "Not by you nor any other shanty Irishman!"

Laura hardly heard what Mr. Clancy said then. She
wanted desperately to be somewhere else. But Mrs.
White told her to come along to dinner. They went
into the kitchen behind the store, and Mr. Clancy
came raging after them.

The kitchen was hot and crowded and cluttered.
Mrs. Clancy was putting dinner on the table, and
three little girls and a boy were pushing each other off
their chairs. Mr. and Mrs. Clancy and Mrs. White, all
quarreling at the top of their voices, sat down and ate
heartily. Laura could not even understand what they
were quarreling about. She could not tell whether Mr.
Clancy was quarreling with his wife or her mother, nor
whether they were quarreling with him or with each
other.

They seemed so angry that she was afraid they
would strike each other. Then Mr. Clancy would say,
"Pass the bread," or, "Fill up this cup, will you?" Mrs.
Clancy would do it, while they went on calling each

other names, yelling them. The children paid no attention. Laura was so upset that she could not eat, she wanted only to get away. She went back to her work as soon as she could.

Mr. Clancy came from the kitchen whistling a tune, as if he had just had a nice, quiet dinner with his family. He asked Mrs. White cheerfully, "How long'll it take to finish those shirts?"

"Not more than a couple of hours," Mrs. White promised. "We'll both work on them."

Laura thought of Ma's saying, "It takes all kinds of people to make a world."

In two hours they finished the four shirts. Laura basted the collars carefully; collars are hard to set properly onto a shirt. Mrs. White sewed them on the machine. Then there were the cuffs to set on the sleeves, and the narrow hems all around the shirt bottoms to be done. Then the fronts, and the cuff openings, were to be faced. There were all the small buttons to sew firmly on, and the buttonholes to be made.

It is not easy to space buttonholes exactly the same distance apart, and it is very difficult to cut them precisely the right size. The tiniest slip of the scissors will make the hole too large, and even one thread uncut will leave it too small.

When she had cut the buttonholes, Laura whipped the cut edges swiftly, and swiftly covered them with the small, knotted stitches, all precisely the same length and closely set together. She so hated making buttonholes that she had learned to do them quickly, and get it over with. Mrs. White noticed her work, and said, "You can beat me making buttonholes."

After those four shirts were done, there were only three more hours of work that day. Laura went on finishing shirts, while Mrs. White cut out more.

Laura had never sat still so long. Her shoulders ached, her neck ached, her fingers were roughened by needle pricks and her eyes were hot and blurry. Twice she had to take out bastings and do them over. She was glad to stand up and fold her work when Pa came in.

They walked briskly home together. The whole day had gone and now the sun was setting.

"How did you like your first day of working for pay, Half-Pint?" Pa asked her. "You make out all right?"

"I think so," she answered. "Mrs. White spoke well of my buttonholes."

THE MONTH OF ROSES

All through that lovely month of June, Laura sewed shirts. Wild roses were blooming in great sweeps of pink through the prairie grasses, but Laura saw them only in the early mornings when she and Pa were hurrying to work.

The soft morning sky was changing to a clearer blue, and already a few wisps of summer cloud were trailing across it. The roses scented the wind, and along the road the fresh blossoms, with their new petals and golden centers, looked up like little faces.

At noon, she knew, great white cloud-puffs would be sailing in sparkling blue. Their shadows would drift across blowing grasses and fluttering roses. But at noon she would be in the noisy kitchen.

At night when she came home, the morning's roses were faded and their petals were scattering on the wind.

Still, she was too old now to play any more. And it was wonderful to think that already she was earning good wages. Every Saturday night Mrs. White counted out a dollar and a half, and Laura took it home to Ma.

"I don't like to take all your money, Laura," Ma said once. "It does seem that you should keep some for yourself."

"Why, Ma, what for?" Laura asked. "I don't need anything."

Her shoes were still good; she had stockings and underwear and her calico dress was almost new. All the week, she looked forward to the pleasure of bringing home her wages to Ma. Often she thought, too, that this was only the beginning.

In two more years she would be sixteen, old enough to teach school. If she studied hard and faithfully, and got a teacher's certificate, and then got a school to teach, she would be a real help to Pa and Ma. Then she could begin to repay them for all that it had cost to provide for her since she was a baby. Then, surely, they could send Mary to college.

Sometimes she almost asked Ma if they could not somehow manage to send Mary to college now, counting on her earnings later to help keep Mary there. She never quite spoke of it, for fear that Ma would say it was too great a chance to take.

Still, the faint hope kept her going more cheerfully to town to work. Her wages were a help. She knew that Ma saved every penny that could be saved, and Mary would go to college as soon as Pa and Ma could possibly send her.

The town was like a sore on the beautiful, wild prairie. Old haystacks and manure piles were rotting around the stables, the backs of the stores' false fronts were rough and ugly. The grass was worn now even from Second Street, and gritty dust blew between the buildings. The town smelled of staleness and dust and smoke and a fatty odor of cooking. A dank smell came from the saloons and a musty sourness from the ground by the back doors where the dishwater was thrown out. But after you had been in town a little while you did not smell its smells, and there was some interest in seeing strangers go by.

The boys and girls that Laura had met in town last winter were not there now. They had gone out to stay on homestead claims. The storekeepers stayed in town to run their stores and bach in the rooms behind them, while wives and children lived all summer out on the prairie in claim shanties. For the law was that a man could not keep a homestead claim unless his family lived on it, six months of every year for five years. Also he must keep ten acres of the sod broken up and planted to crops for five years, before the Government would give him a title to the land. But nobody could make a living from that wild land. So the women and girls stayed all summer in claim shanties to satisfy the law, and the boys broke the sod and planted crops, while the fathers built the town and tried to make money enough to buy food and tools from the East.

The more Laura saw of the town, the more she realized how well off her own family was. That was because Pa had got a whole year's start ahead of the others. He had broken sod last year. Now they had the garden, and the oatfield, and the second planting of corn was growing quite well in the sod. Hay would feed the stock through the winter, and Pa could sell the corn and oats, to buy coal. All the new settlers were beginning now where Pa had begun a year ago.

When Laura looked up from her work she could see almost the whole town, because nearly all the buildings were in the two blocks across the street. All their false fronts stood up, square-cornered at different heights, trying to make believe that the buildings were two stories high.

Mead's Hotel at the end of the street, and Beardsley's Hotel almost opposite Laura, and Tinkham's Furniture Store near the middle of the next block, really did have two stories. Curtains fluttered at their upstairs windows and showed how honest those buildings were, in that row of false fronts.

That was the only difference between them and the other buildings. They were all of pine lumber beginning to weather gray. Each building had two tall glass windows in its front, and a door between them. Every door was open to the warm weather, and every doorway was filled with a strip of faded pink mosquito netting tacked onto a framework to make a screen door.

In front of them all ran the level board sidewalk, and all along its edge were hitching posts. There were always a few horses in sight, tied here and there to the posts, and sometimes a wagon with a team of horses or oxen.

Once in a while, when she bit off a thread, Laura saw a man cross the sidewalk, untie his horse, swing onto it and ride away. Sometimes she heard a team and wagon, and when the sounds were loudest she glanced up and saw it passing by.

One day an outburst of confused shouting startled her. She saw a tall man come bursting out of Brown's saloon. The screen door loudly slammed shut behind him.

With great dignity the man turned about. He looked haughtily at the screen door, and lifting one long leg he thrust his foot contemptuously through the pink mosquito netting. It tore jaggedly from top to bottom. A yell of protest came out of the saloon.

The tall man paid no attention whatever to the yell. He turned haughtily away, and saw in front of him a round little short man. The short man wanted to go into the saloon. The tall man wanted to walk away. But each was in front of the other.

The tall man stood very tall and dignified. The short man stood puffed out with dignity.

In the doorway the saloonkeeper complained about the torn screen door. Neither of them paid any attention to him. They looked at each other and grew more and more dignified.

Suddenly the tall man knew what to do. He linked his long arm in the little man's fat arm, and they came down the sidewalk together, singing.

> "Pull for the shore, sailor!
> Pull for the shore!
> Heed not the stormy winds—"

The tall man solemnly lifted his long leg and thrust his foot through Harthorn's screen door. A yell came out. "Hey, there! What the—"

The two men came on, singing.

> "Though loudly they roar!
> Pull for the shore, sailor—"

They were as dignified as could be. The tall man's long legs made the longest possible steps. The puffed-out little man tried with dignity to stretch his short legs to steps as long.

"Heed not the stormy winds—"

The tall man gravely thrust his foot through the mosquito-netting door of Beardsley's Hotel. Mr. Beardsley came boiling out. The man marched solemnly on.

"Though loudly they roar!"

Laura was laughing so that tears ran out of her eyes. She saw the long, solemn leg rip the mosquito netting in the door of Barker's grocery. Mr. Barker popped out, protesting. The long legs stalking and the fat short legs gravely stretching went away from him haughtily.

"Pull for the shore!"

The tall man's foot pushed through the screen door of Wilder's Feed Store. Royal Wilder yanked it open and said what he thought.

The two men stood listening gravely until he stopped for breath. Then the fat little man said with great dignity, "My name is Tay Pay Pryor and I'm drunk."

They went on, arm in arm, chanting those words.

First the pudgy little man,

"My name is Tay Pay Pryor—"

Then both of them together, like bullfrogs,

"—and I'm drunk!"

The tall man would not say that his name was T. P. Pryor but he always came in solemnly, "—and I'm *DRUNK!*"

They wheeled square about and marched into the other saloon. Its screen door slammed loudly behind them. Laura held her breath, but that one door's mosquito netting stayed smooth and whole.

Laura laughed till her sides ached. She could not stop when Mrs. White snapped out that it was a disgrace to snakes, what men would do with liquor in them.

"Think of the cost of all those screen doors," Mrs. White said. "I'm surprised at you. Young folks nowadays seem to have no realizing sense."

That evening when Laura tried to describe those two men so that Mary could see them, no one laughed.

"Goodness gracious, Laura. How could you laugh at drunken men?" Ma wanted to know.

"I think it is dreadful," Mary added.

Pa said, "The tall one was Bill O'Dowd. I know for

a fact that his brother brought him to a claim out here, to keep him from drinking. Two saloons in this town are just two saloons too many."

"It's a pity more men don't say the same," said Ma. "I begin to believe that if there isn't a stop put to the liquor traffic, women must bestir themselves and have something to say about it."

Pa twinkled at her. "Seems to me you have plenty to say, Caroline. Ma never left me in doubt as to the evil of drink, nor you either."

"Be that as it may be," said Ma. "It's a crying shame that such things can happen before Laura's very eyes."

Pa looked at Laura, and his eyes were still twinkling. Laura knew that he didn't blame her for laughing.

NINE DOLLARS

Mr. Clancy was not getting so many orders for shirts. It seemed that most of the men who could buy shirts that year had bought them. One Saturday evening Mrs. White said, "The spring rush seems to be over."

"Yes, ma'am," said Laura.

Mrs. White counted out a dollar and fifty cents and gave it to her. "I won't be needing you any more, so you needn't come in Monday morning," she said. "Good-by."

"Good-by," Laura said.

She had worked six weeks and earned nine dollars. One dollar had seemed a great deal of money only six weeks ago, but now nine dollars was not enough. If she could have earned only one more week's wages, that would have made ten dollars and a half, or two weeks would have made a whole twelve dollars.

She knew how good it would be to stay at home again, to help with the housework and do the chores and work in the garden, to go walking with Mary and gather wild flowers, and to look forward to Pa's home-coming at night. But somehow she felt cast out, and hollow inside.

Slowly she went along the path beside Main Street. Pa was working now on the building at the corner of Second. He stood by a stack of shingles, waiting for Laura, and when he saw her he sang out, "Look what we've got, to take home to your Ma!"

In the shade of the shingles stood a bushel bas-ket covered with a grain sack. Inside it there was a small rasping of claws, and a cheeping chorus. The chickens!

"Boast brought 'em in today," said Pa. "Fourteen of 'em, all healthy and thriving." His whole face was beaming with anticipation of Ma's delight.

He told Laura, "The basket's not heavy. You take one handle and I'll take the other, and we'll carry them level, between us."

They went down Main Street and out on the road toward home, carrying the basket carefully between them. Sunset was flaming in crimson and burning gold over the whole sky. The air was filled with golden light and Silver Lake to the east was blazing like fire. Up from the basket came the chickens' wondering and anxious cheeping.

"Pa, Mrs. White doesn't want me any more," Laura said.

"Yes, I guess the spring rush is about over," said Pa.

Laura had not thought that Pa's job might end.

"Oh, Pa, won't there be any more carpentering, either?" she asked.

"We couldn't expect it to last all summer," said Pa. "Anyway, I'll have to be making hay pretty soon."

After a while Laura said, "I only earned nine dollars, Pa."

"Nine dollars is nothing to sneeze at," said Pa. "You've done good work, too, and fully satisfied Mrs. White, haven't you?"

"Yes," Laura answered honestly.

"Then it's a good job well done," said Pa.

It was true that that was some satisfaction. Laura felt a little better. Besides, they were taking the chickens to Ma.

Ma was delighted when she saw them. Carrie and Grace crowded to peep at them in the basket, and Laura told Mary about them. They were healthy, lively chicks, with bright black eyes and bright yellow claws. Already the down was coming off them, leaving naked patches on their necks, and the sprouting feathers were showing on their wings and tails. They were every color that chickens are, and some were spotted.

Ma lifted each one carefully into her apron. "Mrs.

Boast can't have got these all from one hatching," she said. "I do believe there's not more than two cockerels among them."

"The Boasts have got such a head-start with chickens, likely they're planning to eat friers this summer," said Pa. "It may be she took a few cockerels out of this flock, looking on them as meat."

"Yes, and replaced them with pullets that will be layers," Ma guessed. "It would be Mrs. Boast all over. A more generous woman never lived."

She carried the chicks in her apron, to set them one by one into the coop that Pa had already made. It had a front of laths, to let in air and sun, and a little door with a wooden button to fasten it. It had no floor, but was set on clean grass that the chicks could eat, and when the grass grew trampled and dirty, the coop could be moved to fresh grass.

In an old pie pan Ma mixed a crumbly bran mash, well peppered. She set it in the coop, and the chicks crowded onto it, gobbling the bran mash so greedily that sometimes they tried to swallow their own toes by mistake. When they could eat no more, they perched on the edge of the water pan, and scooping up water in their beaks they stretched up their necks and tilted back their heads, to swallow it.

Ma said it would be Carrie's task to feed them often and to keep their water pan filled with cool, fresh water. Tomorrow she would let the chicks out to run, and it would be Grace's part to keep a sharp lookout for hawks.

After supper that evening she sent Laura to make sure that the chicks were sleeping safely. All the stars were shining over the dark prairie and a sickle moon was low in the west. The grasses were breathing softly, asleep in the quiet night.

Laura's hand felt gently over the sleeping chicks, huddled warm together in a corner of the coop. Then she stood looking at the summer night. She did not know how long she had stood there, until she saw Ma coming from the house.

"Oh, there you are, Laura," Ma softly said. As Laura had done, she knelt and put her hand through the coop's door to feel the huddled chicks. Then she, too, stood looking.

"The place begins to look like a farm," she said. The oatfield and the cornfield were shadowy pale in the darkness, and the garden was bumpy with lumps of dark leaves. Like pools of faint star-shine among them spread the cucumber vines and the pumpkins. The low sod stable could hardly be seen, but from the house window a warm yellow light shone out.

Suddenly, without thinking at all, Laura said, "Oh, Ma, I do wish Mary could go to college this fall."

Unexpectedly Ma replied, "It may be that she can. Your Pa and I have been talking of it."

Laura could not speak for a minute. Then she asked, "Have you—have you said anything to her?"

"Not yet," said Ma. "We must not raise hopes only to be disappointed. But with Pa's wages, and the oats and the corn, if nothing goes wrong, we think she can go this fall. We must trust ourselves to contrive to

61

keep her there till she finishes the full seven years' course, both college and manual training."

Then for the first time Laura realized that when Mary went to college, she would go away. Mary would be gone. All day long, Mary would not be there. Laura could not think what living would be, without Mary.

"Oh, I wish—" she began, and stopped. She had been so eagerly hoping that Mary could go to college.

"Yes, we will miss her," Ma said steadily. "But we must think what a great opportunity it will be for her."

"I know, Ma," Laura said miserably.

The night was large and empty now. The light shining from the house was warm and steady, but even home would not be the same when Mary was not there.

Then Ma said, "Your nine dollars are a great help, Laura. I have been planning, and I do believe that with nine dollars I can buy the goods for Mary's best dress, and perhaps the velvet to make her a hat."

FOURTH OF JULY

BOOM!
Laura was jerked out of sleep. The bedroom was dark. Carrie asked in a thin, scared whisper, "What was that?"

"Don't be scared," Laura answered. They listened. The window was hardly gray in the dark, but Laura could feel that the middle of the night was past.

BOOM! The air seemed to shake.

"Great guns!" Pa exclaimed sleepily.

"Why? Why?" Grace demanded. "Pa, Ma, why?"

Carrie asked, "Who is it? What are they shooting?"

"What time is it?" Ma wanted to know.

Through the partition Pa answered, "It's Fourth of July, Carrie." The air shook again. BOOM!

It was not great guns. It was gunpowder exploded under the blacksmith's anvil, in town. The noise was like the noise of battles that Americans fought for independence. Fourth of July was the day when the first Americans declared that all men are born free and equal. BOOM!

"Come, girls, we might as well get up," Ma called.

Pa sang, "'Oh, say, can you see, by the dawn's early light?'"

"Charles!" Ma protested, but she was laughing, because it really was too dark to see.

"It's nothing to be solemn about!" Pa jumped out of bed. "Hurray! We're Americans!" He sang:

> "Hurray! Hurray! We'll sing the jubilee!
> Hurray! Hurray! The flag that sets men free!"

Even the sun, as it rose shining into the clearest of skies, seemed to know this day was the glorious Fourth. At breakfast Ma said, "This would be a perfect day for a Fourth of July picnic."

"Maybe the town'll be far enough along to have one, come next July," said Pa.

"We couldn't hardly have a picnic this year, anyway," Ma admitted. "It wouldn't seem like a picnic, without fried chicken."

After such a rousing beginning, the day did seem empty. Such a special day seemed to expect some special happening, but nothing special could happen.

"I feel like dressing up," Carrie said while they did the dishes.

"So do I, but there's nothing to dress up for," Laura replied.

When she carried out the dishwater to throw it far from the house, she saw Pa looking at the oats. They were growing thick and tall, gray-green and smoothly rippling in the wind. The corn was growing lustily, too. Its long, yellow-green, fluttering leaves almost hid the broken sod. In the garden the cucumber vines were reaching out, their crawling tips uncurling beyond patches of spreading big leaves. The rows of peas and beans were rounding up, the carrot rows were feathery green and the beets were thrusting up long, dark leaves on red stems. The ground-cherries were already small bushes. Through the wild grasses the chickens were scattered, chasing insects to eat.

All this was satisfaction enough for an ordinary day, but for Fourth of July there should be something more.

Pa felt the same way. He had nothing to do, for on Fourth of July no work could be done except the chores and housework. In a little while he came into the house and said to Ma, "There's a kind of celebration in town today, would you like to go?"

"What kind of celebration?" Ma asked.

"Well, mostly horse racing, but they took up a

collection for lemonade," Pa replied.

"Women are not likely to be at a horse race," Ma said. "And I couldn't go calling, uninvited, on Fourth of July."

Laura and Carrie stood almost bursting with eagerness while Ma considered, and shook her head. "You go along, Charles. It would be too much for Grace, anyway."

"It is much nicer at home," said Mary.

Then Laura spoke. "Oh Pa, if you go, can't Carrie and I?"

Pa's doubtful eyes brightened, and twinkled at her and Carrie. Ma smiled on them.

"Yes, Charles, it will be a nice outing for you all," she said. "Run down cellar and bring up the butter, Carrie, and while you're dressing I'll put up some bread-and-butter for you to take along."

Suddenly the day seemed really Fourth of July. Ma made sandwiches, Pa blacked his boots, Laura and Carrie hurriedly dressed up. Luckily Laura's sprigged calico was freshly washed and ironed. She and Carrie took turns scrubbing their faces and necks and ears pink. Over their unbleached muslin union suits they put on crackling stiff petticoats of bleached muslin. They brushed and braided their hair. Laura wound her heavy braids around her head and pinned them. She tied the Sunday hair ribbon on the ends of Carrie's braids. Then she put on her fresh sprigged calico and buttoned it up the back. The full ruffle on the bottom of the full skirt came down to the tops of her shoes.

"Please button me up," Carrie asked. In the middle of her back there were two buttons that she couldn't reach. She had buttoned all the others outside-in.

"You can't wear your buttons turned inside, at a Fourth of July celebration," said Laura, unbuttoning them all and buttoning them again properly.

"If they're outside, they keep pulling my hair," Carrie protested. "My braids catch on them."

"I know. Mine always did," said Laura. "But you just have to stand it till you're big enough to put your hair up."

They put on their sunbonnets. Pa was waiting, holding the brown-paper packet of sandwiches. Ma looked at them carefully and said, "You look very nice."

"It's a treat to me, to be stepping out with my two good-looking girls," said Pa.

"You look nice, too, Pa," Laura told him. His boots were glossily polished, his beard was trimmed, and he was wearing his Sunday suit and broad-brimmed felt hat.

"I want to go!" Grace demanded. Even when Ma said "No, Grace," she repeated two or three times, "I want to!" Because she was the baby, they had almost spoiled her. Now her unruliness must be nipped in the bud. Pa had to set her sternly in a chair and tell her, "You heard your Ma speak."

They set out soberly, unhappy about Grace. But she must be taught to mind. Perhaps next year she could go, if there were a big celebration and they all rode in the wagon. Now they were walking, to let the horses stay on their picket ropes and eat grass. Horses grow tired, standing all day at hitching posts in dust and heat. Grace was too little to walk the mile and back, and she was too big to be carried.

Even before they reached town, they could hear a sound like corn popping. Carrie asked what it was, and Pa said it was firecrackers.

Horses were tied along the whole length of Main Street. Men and boys were so thick on the sidewalk that in places they almost touched each other. Boys were throwing lighted firecrackers into the dusty street, where they sizzled and exploded. The noise was startling.

"I didn't know it would be like this," Carrie murmured. Laura did not like it, either. They had never been in such a crowd before. There was nothing to do but keep on walking up and down in it, and to be among so many strangers made them uncomfortable.

Twice they walked the two blocks with Pa, and then Laura asked him if she and Carrie could not stay in his store building. Pa said that was a fine idea. They could watch the crowd while he circulated a little; then they would eat their lunch and see the races. He

let them into the empty building and Laura shut the door.

It was pleasant to be alone in the echoing bare place. They looked at the empty kitchen behind it, where they had all lived huddled during the long hard winter. They tiptoed upstairs to the hollow, hot bedrooms under the eaves of the shingle roof, and stood looking down from the front window at the crowd, and at firecrackers squirming and popping in the dust.

"I wish we had some firecrackers," Carrie said.

"They're guns," Laura pretended. "We're in Fort Ticonderoga, and those are British and Indians. We're Americans, fighting for independence."

"It was the British in Fort Ticonderoga, and the Green Mountain boys took it," Carrie objected.

"Then I guess we're with Daniel Boone in Kentucky, and this is a log stockade," said Laura. "Only the British and Indians captured him," she had to admit.

"How much do firecrackers cost?" Carrie asked.

"Even if Pa could afford them, it's foolish to spend money just to make a little noise," Laura said. "Look at that little bay pony. Let's pick out the horses we like best; you can have first choice."

There was so much to see that they could hardly believe it was noon when Pa's boots sounded downstairs and he called, "Girls! Where are you?"

They rushed down. He was having a good time, his

eyes were twinkling bright. He sang out, "I've brought us a treat! Smoked herring, to go with our bread and butter! And look what else!" He showed them a bunch of firecrackers.

"Oh, Pa!" Carrie cried. "How much did they cost?"

"Didn't cost me a cent," said Pa. "Lawyer Barnes handed them to me, said to give them to you girls."

"Why on earth did he do that?" Laura asked. She had never heard of Lawyer Barnes before.

"Oh, he's going in for politics, I guess," said Pa. "He acts that way, affable and agreeable to everybody. You want me to set these off for you now, or after we eat?"

Laura and Carrie were thinking the same thing. They knew it when they looked at each other, and Carrie said it. "Let's save them, Pa, to take home to Grace."

"All right," said Pa. He put them in his pocket and undid the smoked herring while Laura opened the packet of sandwiches. The herring was delicious. They saved some to take home to Ma. When they had eaten the last bit of bread and butter they went out to the well and drank, long and deep, from the edge of the pail that Pa drew dripping up. Then they washed their hands and their hot faces and dried them on Pa's handkerchief.

It was time to go to the races. The whole crowd was moving across the railroad tracks and out on the prairie. On a pole set up there, the American flag fluttered against the sky. The sun was shining warm and a cool breeze was blowing.

Beside the flagpole a man rose up tall above the crowd. He was standing on something. The sound of talking died down, and he could be heard speaking.

"Well, boys," he said, "I'm not much good at public speaking, but today's the glorious Fourth. This is the day and date when our forefathers cut loose from the despots of Europe. There wasn't many Americans at that time, but they wouldn't stand for any monarch tyrannizing over them. They had to fight the British regulars and their hired Hessians and the murdering scalping red-skinned savages that those fine gold-laced aristocrats turned loose on our settlements and paid for murdering and burning and scalping women and children. A few barefoot Americans had to fight the whole of them and lick 'em, and they did fight them and they did lick them. Yes sir! We licked the British in 1776 and we licked 'em again in 1812, and we backed all the monarchies of Europe out of Mexico and off this continent less than twenty years ago, and by glory! Yessir, by Old Glory right here, waving over my head, any time the despots of Europe try to step on America's toes, we'll lick 'em again!"

"Hurray! Hurray!" everybody shouted. Laura and Carrie and Pa yelled, too, "Hurray! Hurray!"

"Well, so here we are today," the man went on.

"Every man Jack of us a free and independent citizen of God's country, the only country on earth where a man is free and independent. Today's the Fourth of July, when this whole thing was started, and it ought to have a bigger, better celebration than this. We can't do much this year. Most of us are out here trying to pull ourselves up by our own boot straps. By next year, likely some of us will be better off, and be able to chip in for a real big rousing celebration of Independence Day. Meantime, here we are. It's Fourth of July, and on this day somebody's got to read the Declaration of Independence. It looks like I'm elected, so hold your hats, boys; I'm going to read it."

Laura and Carrie knew the Declaration by heart, of course, but it gave them a solemn, glorious feeling to hear the words. They took hold of hands and stood listening in the solemnly listening crowd. The Stars and Stripes were fluttering bright against the thin, clear blue overhead, and their minds were saying the words before their ears heard them.

"When in the course of human events it becomes necessary for one people to dissolve the political bonds which have connected them with another, and to assume among the powers of the earth the separate and equal station to which the laws of Nature and of Nature's God entitle them, a decent respect to the opinions of mankind requires that they should declare the causes which impel them to the separation.

"We hold these truths to be self-evident, that all men are created equal, that they are endowed by their Creator with certain inalienable rights, that among these are Life, Liberty, and the pursuit of Happiness. . . ."

Then came the long and terrible list of the crimes of the King.

"He has endeavored to prevent the population of these States.

"He has obstructed the administration of Justice.

"He has made Judges dependent on his will alone.

"He has erected a multitude of new offices, and sent hither swarms of officers to harass our people and to eat out their substance.

"He has plundered our seas, ravaged our coasts, burnt our towns, and destroyed the lives of our people . . .

"He is at this time transporting large Armies of foreign Mercenaries to complete the works of death, destruction and tyranny, already begun with circumstances of cruelty and perfidy scarcely paralleled in the most barbarous ages, and totally unworthy the head of a civilized nation. . . .

"We, therefore, the Representatives of the United States of America, in General Congress assembled, appealing to the Supreme Judge of the world for the rectitude of our intentions, do, in the name and by the authority of the good People of these Colonies, solemnly publish and declare,

"That these United Colonies are, and of right ought to be, Free and Independent States, that they are absolved from all allegiance to the British Crown, and that all political connection between them and the State of Great Britain is and ought to be totally dissolved; and that as Free and Independent States, they have full right to levy War . . .

"And for the support of this Declaration, with a firm reliance on the protection of Divine Providence, we mutually pledge to each other our Lives, our Fortunes, and our sacred Honor."

No one cheered. It was more like a moment to say, "Amen." But no one quite knew what to do.

Then Pa began to sing. All at once everyone was singing:

> "My country, 'tis of thee,
> Sweet land of liberty,
> Of thee I sing. . . .
>
> "Long may our land be bright
> With Freedom's holy light,
> Protect us by Thy might,
> Great God, our King!"

The crowd was scattering away then, but Laura stood stock still. Suddenly she had a completely new thought. The Declaration and the song came together in her mind, and she thought: God is America's king.

She thought: Americans won't obey any king on earth. Americans are free. That means they have to obey their own consciences. No king bosses Pa; he has to boss himself. Why (she thought), when I am a little older, Pa and Ma will stop telling me what to do, and there isn't anyone else who has a right to give me orders. I will have to make myself be good.

Her whole mind seemed to be lighted up by that thought. This is what it means to be free. It means, you have to be good. "Our father's God, author of liberty—" The laws of Nature and of Nature's God endow you with a right to life and liberty. Then you have to keep the laws of God, for God's law is the only thing that gives you a right to be free.

Laura had no time then to think any further. Carrie was wondering why she stood so still, and Pa was saying, "This way, girls! There's the free lemonade!"

The barrels stood in the grass by the flagpole. A few men were waiting for their turns to drink from the tin dipper. As each finished drinking, he handed the dipper on, and then strolled away toward the horses and buggies on the race track.

Laura and Carrie hung back a little, but the man who had the dipper saw them and handed the dipper to Pa. He filled it from the barrel and gave it to Carrie. The barrel was almost full, and slices of lemon floated thick on the lemonade.

"I see they put in plenty of lemons, so it ought to be

good," Pa said, while Carrie slowly drank. Her eyes grew round with delight; she had never tasted lemonade before.

"They've just mixed it," one of the waiting men told Pa. "The water is fresh from the hotel well, so it's cold."

Another man who was waiting said, "It depends, some, on how much sugar they put in."

Pa filled the dipper again and gave it to Laura. She had once tasted lemonade, at Nellie Oleson's party, when she was a little girl in Minnesota. This lemonade was even more delicious. She drank the last drop from the dipper and thanked Pa. It would not be polite to ask for more. When Pa had drunk, they went across the trampled grass to the crowd by the race track. A great ring of sod had been broken, and the sod carried off. The breaking plow with its coulter had left the black earth smooth and level. In the middle of the ring and all around it the prairie grasses were waving, except where men and buggies had made trampled tracks.

"Why, hello, Boast!" Pa called, and Mr. Boast came through the crowd. He had just got to town in time for the races. Mrs. Boast, like Ma, had preferred to stay at home.

Four ponies came out on the track. There were two bay ponies, one gray, and one black. The boys who were riding them lined them up in a straight row.

"Which'd you bet on, if you were betting?" Mr. Boast asked.

"Oh, the black one!" Laura cried. The black pony's coat shone in the sunlight and its long mane and tail blew silky on the breeze. It tossed its slender head and picked up its feet daintily.

At the word, "Go!" all the ponies leaped into a run. The crowd yelled. Stretched out low and fast, the black pony went by, the others behind it. All their pounding feet raised a cloud of dust that hid them. Then around the far side of the track they went, running with all their might. The gray pony crept up beside the black. Neck and neck they were running, then the gray pulled a little ahead and the crowd yelled again. Laura still hoped for the black. It was doing its best. Little by little it gained on the gray. Its head passed the gray's neck, its outstretched nose was almost even with the gray's nose. Suddenly all four ponies were coming head-on down the track, quickly growing larger and larger in front of the on-coming dust. The bay pony with the white nose came skimming past the black and the gray, across the line ahead of them both while the crowd cheered.

"If you'd bet on the black, Laura, you'd've lost," said Pa.

"It's the prettiest, though," Laura answered. She had never been so excited. Carrie's eyes shone, her

LITTLE TOWN ON THE PRAIRIE

cheeks were pink with excitement; her braid was snared on a button and recklessly she yanked it loose.

"Are there any more, Pa? more races?" Carrie cried.

"Sure, here they come for the buggy race," Pa answered. Mr. Boast joked, "Pick the winning team, Laura!"

Through the crowd and out onto the track came first a bay team hitched to a light buggy. The bays were perfectly matched and they stepped as though the buggy weighed nothing at all. Then came other teams, other buggies, but Laura hardly saw them, for there was a team of brown horses that she knew. She knew their proud, gay heads and arching necks, the shine of light on their satiny shoulders, the black manes blowing and the forelocks tossing above their quick, bright, gentle eyes.

"Oh, look, Carrie, look! It's the brown Morgans!" she cried.

"That's Almanzo Wilder's team, Boast," said Pa. "What in creation has he got 'em hitched to?"

High up above the horses, Almanzo Wilder was sitting. His hat was pushed back on his head and he looked cheerful and confident.

He turned the team toward its place in line, and they saw that he was sitting on a high seat, on top of a long, high, heavy wagon, with a door in its side.

"It's his brother Royal's peddler's wagon," said a man standing near by.

"He don't have a chance, with that weight, against all those light buggies," said another. Everyone was looking at the Morgans and the wagon and talking about them.

"The off horse, Prince, is the one he drove last winter, that forty-mile trip that he and Cap Garland made, and brought in the wheat that kept us all from starving to death," Pa told Mr. Boast. "The other one's Lady, that ran off with the antelope herd that time. They've both got good action, and speed."

"I see that," Mr. Boast agreed. "But no team can haul that heavy cart and beat Sam Owen's bays on his light buggy. Seems like the young fellow might have rousted out a buggy somewheres in this country."

"He's an independent kind of a young cuss," someone said. "He'd rather lose with what he's got than win with a borrowed buggy."

"Too bad he don't own a buggy," Mr. Boast said.

The brown horses were by far the most beautiful on the track, and so proud. They did not seem to mind the heavy wagon at all, but tossed their heads, pricked their ears, and lifted their feet as if the ground were not quite good enough for them to step on.

"Oh, what a shame, what a *shame* they haven't a fair chance," Laura was thinking. Her hands were clenched. She wished so much that those proud, fine horses might only have a fair chance. Hitched to that heavy wagon, they could not win. She cried out, "Oh, it isn't *fair!*"

The race started. Fast came the bays, leading all the others. The shining legs trotting and the wheels whirling hardly seemed to touch the ground. Every buggy rushing by was a light, one-seated buggy. Not a team drew even the weight of a two-seated buggy, except the beautiful brown horses who came last, pulling the high, heavy peddler's cart.

"Best team in the country," Laura heard a man say, "but not a chance."

"Nope," said another. "That wagon's too heavy for them to pull. Sure as shooting, they'll break their trot."

But they were pulling it, and they were trotting. Evenly, without a break, the eight brown legs kept moving in a perfect trot. The dust-cloud rose up and hid them. Then bursting out of it, up the other side of the track the teams and buggies were speeding. One buggy— No, two buggies! were behind the peddler's cart. Three buggies were behind it. Only the bays were ahead of it.

"Oh, come on! Come on! Win Win!" Laura was begging the brown horses. She so wanted them to trot faster that it seemed her wishing was pulling them.

They were almost around the track. They were coming now around the turn and on toward the line.

The bays were ahead. The Morgans could not do it, they could not win, the weight was too much for them, but still Laura kept on wishing with all of her. "Faster, faster, only a little faster. Oh, come on, come *on!*"

Almanzo leaned forward from the high seat and seemed to speak to them. Still smoothly trotting, they came faster. Their heads reached Mr. Owen's buggy and slowly, smoothly crept by it. All the legs were moving fast, fast, while so slowly the brown heads came up, even with the bays'. All four horses were coming now in a line, faster, faster.

"A tie. By gosh, it's a tie," a man said.

Then Mr. Owen's buggy whip flashed out. It swished down, once, twice, as he shouted. The bays leaped ahead. Almanzo had no whip. He was leaning forward, lightly holding the reins firm. Once more he seemed to speak. Fast and smooth as swallows flying, the brown Morgans passed the bays and crossed the line. They'd won!

The whole crowd shouted. It surged to surround the brown horses and Almanzo high on the cart. Laura found that she had been holding her breath. Her knees were wobbly. She wanted to yell and to laugh and to cry and to sit down and rest.

"Oh, they won! they won! they won!" Carrie kept saying, clapping her hands. Laura did not say anything.

"He earned that five dollars," said Mr. Boast.

"What five dollars?" Carrie asked.

"Some men in town put up five dollars for the best trotting team," Pa explained. "Almanzo Wilder's won it."

Laura was glad she had not known. She could not have borne it if she had known that the brown horses were running for a five-dollar prize.

"He has it coming to him," said Pa. "That young man knows how to handle horses."

There were no more races. There was nothing more to do but stand around and listen to the talking. The lemonade was low in the barrel. Mr. Boast brought Laura and Carrie a dipperful and they divided it. It was sweeter than before, but not so cold. The teams and buggies were going away. Then Pa came from the dwindling crowd and said it was time to go home.

Mr. Boast walked with them along Main Street. Pa said to him that the Wilders had a sister who was a schoolteacher back east in Minnesota. "She's taken a claim half a mile west of town here," said Pa, "and she wants Almanzo to find out if she can get this school to teach next winter. I told him to tell her to send in her application to the school board. Other things being equal, I don't know why she can't as well have it."

Laura and Carrie looked at each other. Pa was on

the school board, and no doubt the others would feel as he did. Laura thought, "Maybe if I am a very good scholar and if she likes me, maybe she might take me driving behind those beautiful horses."

BLACKBIRDS

In August, the days were so hot that Laura and Mary took their walks in the early mornings before the sun had risen far. The air still had some freshness then and it was not too hot to be pleasant. But every walk seemed like a little bit of the last walk they would have together, for soon Mary was going away.

She was really going to college, that fall. They had looked forward so long to her going, that now when she really was going, it did not seem possible. It was hard to imagine, too, because none of them knew what college would be like; they had never seen one. But Pa had earned nearly a hundred dollars that spring; the garden and the oats and the corn were growing marvelously; and Mary really could go to college.

Coming back from their walk one morning, Laura noticed several grasses sticking to Mary's skirt. She tried to pull them off, but they would not come loose.

"Ma!" she called. "Come look at this funny grass." Ma had never seen a grass like it. The grass heads were like barley beards, except that they were twisted, and they ended in a seed pod an inch long, with a point as fine and hard as a needle, and a shaft covered with stiff hairs pointing backward. Like real needles, the points had sewed themselves into Mary's dress. The stiff hair followed the needle-point easily, but kept it from being pulled back, and the four-inch-long, screw-like beard followed, twisting and pushing the needle-point farther in.

"Ouch! something bit me!" Mary exclaimed. Just above her shoetop, one of the strange grasses had pierced her stocking and was screwing itself into her flesh.

"I declare this beats all," said Ma. "What next will we encounter on this homestead?"

When Pa came in at noon, they showed him the strange grass. He said it was Spanish needle grass. When it got in the mouths of horses or cattle, it must be cut out of their lips and tongues. It worked through sheep's wool and into the sheep's bodies, often killing them.

"Where did you girls find it?" he asked, and he was glad that Laura could not tell him. "If you didn't notice it, there can't be much of it. It grows in patches, and spreads. Exactly where did you go walking?"

Laura could tell him that. He said he would attend to that grass. "Some say it can be killed by burning it over, green," he told them. "I'll burn it now, to kill as many seeds as I can, and next spring I'll be on the lookout and burn it, green."

There were little new potatoes for dinner, creamed with green peas, and there were string beans and green onions. And by every plate was a saucer full of sliced tomatoes, to be eaten with sugar and cream.

"Well, we've got good things to eat, and plenty of them," said Pa, taking a second helping of potatoes and peas.

"Yes," Ma said happily; "nowadays we can all eat enough to make up for what we couldn't have last winter."

She was proud of the garden; it was growing so well. "I shall begin salting down cucumbers tomorrow, little ones are thick under all those vines. And the potato tops are thriving so, I can hardly find the hills underneath them, to scrabble."

"If nothing happens to them, we'll have plenty of potatoes this winter!" Pa rejoiced.

"We'll have roasting ears soon, too," Ma announced. "I noticed, this morning, some of the corn silks are beginning to darken."

"I never saw a better corn crop," said Pa. "We've got that to depend on."

"And the oats," said Ma. Then she asked, "What's wrong with the oats, Charles?"

"Well, blackbirds are getting most of them," Pa told her. "I no sooner set up a shock than it's covered thick with the pests. They're eating all the grain they can get at, and not leaving much but the straw."

Ma's cheerful face dimmed, but Pa went on. "Never mind, there's a good crop of straw, and soon as I get the oats cut and shocked I'll clear out the blackbirds with a shotgun."

That afternoon, looking up from her sewing to thread her needle, Laura saw a wisp of smoke wavering in the heat waves from the prairie. Pa had taken time from his work in the oatfield to cut a swath around the patch of Spanish needles and set fire to those vicious grasses.

"The prairie looks so beautiful and gentle," she said. "But I wonder what it will do next. Seems like we have to fight it all the time."

"This earthly life is a battle," said Ma. "If it isn't one thing to contend with, it's another. It always has been so, and it always will be. The sooner you make up your mind to that, the better off you are, and the more thankful for your pleasures. Now Mary, I'm ready to fit the bodice."

They were making Mary's best winter dress, for college. In the hot room, with the sun blazing on the thin board walls and roof, the lapfuls of wool cashmere almost smothered them. Ma was nervous about this best dress. She had made the summer dresses first, for practice with the patterns.

She had cut the patterns from newspaper, using her dressmaker's chart of thin cardboard as a guide. Lines and figures for all different sizes were printed on it. The trouble was that nobody was exactly any of the sizes on the chart. After Ma had measured Mary, and figured and marked the size of every sleeve and skirt and bodice piece on the chart, and cut the patterns, and cut and basted the dress lining, then when she tried the lining on Mary she had to make changes all along the seams.

Laura had never before known that Ma hated sewing. Her gentle face did not show it now, and her voice was never exasperated. But her patience was so tight around her mouth that Laura knew she hated sewing as much as Laura did.

They were worried, too, because while they were buying the dress goods Mrs. White had told them that she had heard from her sister in Iowa that hoop skirts were coming back, in New York. There were no hoops yet to be bought in town, but Mr. Clancy was thinking of ordering some.

"I declare, I don't know," Ma said, worrying about

hoop skirts. Mrs. Boast had had a *Godey's Lady's Book* last year. If she had one now, it would decide the question. But Pa must cut the oats and the hay; they were all too tired on Sundays to make the long, hot trip to the Boasts' claim. When at last Pa saw Mr. Boast in town one Saturday, he said that Mrs. Boast did not have a new *Godey's Lady's Book*.

"We'll just make the skirts wide enough, so if hoops do come back, Mary can buy some in Iowa and wear them," Ma decided. "Meanwhile, her petticoats can hold the skirts out full."

They had made four new petticoats for Mary, two of unbleached muslin, one of bleached muslin, and one of fine white cambric. Around the bottom of the fine cambric one, Laura had sewed with careful, tiny stitches the six yards of knitted lace that she had given Mary for Christmas.

They had made for her two gray flannel petticoats and three red flannel union suits. Around the top of the petticoats' hems, Laura made a row of catch-stitching in bright, red yarn. It was pretty on the gray flannel. She back-stitched all the seams of the petti-coats and the long red flannel union suits, and around the necks and the wrists of the long red sleeves she catch-stitched a trimming of blue yarn.

She was using all the pretty yarns that had come in last winter's Christmas barrel, but she was glad to do it. Not one of the girls in college would have prettier underwear than Mary's.

When Ma had back-stitched the seams of Mary's dresses and carefully ironed them flat, Laura sewed the whalebone stays onto the underarm seams and dart-seams of the basques. She took great pains to sew them evenly on both edges without making the tiniest wrinkle in the seams, so that the basque would fit trimly and smoothly on the outside. This was such anxious work that it made the back of her neck ache.

Now the basque of Mary's best dress was ready to try on for the last time. It was brown cashmere, lined with brown cambric. Small brown buttons buttoned it down the front, and on either side of the buttons and around the bottom Ma had trimmed it with a narrow, shirred strip of brown-and-blue plaid, with red threads and golden threads running through it. A high collar of the plaid was sewed on, and Ma held in her hand a gathered length of white machine-made lace. The lace was to be fitted inside the collar, so that it would fall a little over the top.

"Oh, Mary, it's beautiful. The back fits without a wrinkle, and so do the shoulders," Laura told her. "And the sleeves look absolutely skin tight to the elbows."

"They are," Mary said. "I don't know if I can button—"

Laura went around in front. "Hold your breath, Mary. Breathe out, and hold it," she advised anxiously.

"It's too tight," Ma said in despair. Some of the buttons strained in the buttonholes, some could not be buttoned at all.

"Don't breathe, Mary! Don't breathe!" Laura said frantically, and quickly she unbuttoned the straining buttons. "Now you can." Mary breathed, outbursting from the open bodice.

"Oh, how ever did I make such a mistake," Ma said. "That bodice fitted well enough last week."

Laura had a sudden thought. "It's Mary's corsets! It must be. The corset strings must have stretched."

It was so. When Mary held her breath again and Laura pulled tight the corset strings, the bodice buttoned, and it fitted beautifully.

"I'm glad I don't have to wear corsets yet," said Carrie.

"Be glad while you can be," said Laura. "You'll have to wear them pretty soon." Her corsets were a sad affliction to her, from the time she put them on in the morning until she took them off at night. But when girls pinned up their hair and wore skirts down to their shoetops, they must wear corsets.

"You should wear them all night," Ma said. Mary did, but Laura could not bear at night the torment of the steels that would not let her draw a deep breath. Always before she could get to sleep, she had to take off her corsets.

"What your figure will be, goodness knows," Ma

warned her. "When I was married, your Pa could span my waist with his two hands."

"He can't now," Laura answered, a little saucily. "And he seems to like you."

"You must not be saucy, Laura," Ma reproved her, but Ma's cheeks flushed pink and she could not help smiling.

Now she fitted the white lace into Mary's collar and pinned it so that it fell gracefully over the collar's edge and made a full cascade between the collar's ends in front.

They all stood back to admire. The gored skirt of brown cashmere was smooth and rather tight in front, but gathered full around the sides and back, so that it would be ample for hoops. In front it touched the floor evenly, in back it swept into a graceful short train that swished when Mary turned. All around the bottom was a pleated flounce.

The overskirt was of the brown-and-blue plaid. It was shirred in front, it was draped up at the sides to show more of the skirt beneath, and at the back it fell in rich, full puffs, caught up above the flounced train.

Above all this, Mary's waist rose slim in the tight, smooth bodice. The neat little buttons ran up to the soft white lace cascading under Mary's chin. The brown cashmere was smooth as paint over her sloping shoulders and down to her elbows; then the

sleeves widened. A shirring of the plaid curved around them, and the wide wrists fell open, showing the lining of white lace ruffles that set off Mary's slender hands.

Mary was beautiful in that beautiful dress. Her hair was silkier and more golden than the golden silk threads in the plaid. Her blind eyes were bluer than the blue in it. Her cheeks were pink, and her figure was so stylish.

"Oh, Mary," Laura said. "You look exactly as if you'd stepped out of a fashion plate. There won't be, there just can't be, one single girl in college who can hold a candle to you."

"Do I really look so well, Ma?" Mary asked timidly, and she flushed pinker.

For once Ma did not guard against vanity. "Yes, Mary, you do," she said. "You are not only as stylish as can be, you are beautiful. No matter where you go, you will be a pleasure to every eye that sees you. And, I am thankful to say, you may be sure your clothes are equal to any occasion."

They could not look at her longer. She was almost fainting from the heat, in that woolen dress. They laid it carefully away, done at last, and a great success. There were only a few more things to be done now. Ma must make Mary a winter hat of velvet, and knit some stockings for her, and Laura was knitting her a pair of mitts, of brown silk thread.

"I can finish them in spare time," Laura said. "We're through with the sewing, in time for me to help Pa make hay."

She liked working with Pa, and she liked working outdoors in the sun and wind. Besides, secretly she was hoping to leave off her corsets while she worked in the haying.

"I suppose you may help to load the hay," Ma agreed reluctantly, "but it will be stacked in town."

"Oh, Ma, *no!* Do we have to move to town again?" Laura cried.

"Modulate your voice, Laura," Ma said gently. "Remember, 'Her voice was ever gentle, low, and soft, an excellent thing in woman.'"

"Do we have to go to town?" Laura murmured.

"Your Pa and I think best not to risk a winter in this house until he can make it more weatherproof," said Ma. "You know that we could not have lived through last winter here."

"Maybe this winter won't be so bad," Laura pleaded.

"We must not tempt Providence," Ma said firmly. Laura knew it was decided; they had to live in town again next winter, and she must make the best of it.

That evening when the flock of happy blackbirds was swirling at play in the sunset air above the oat-field, Pa took out his shotgun and shot them. He did not like to do it, and in the house no one liked to hear the shots, but they knew it must be done. Pa must protect the crops. The horses and Ellen and her calves would live on hay that winter, but the oats and the corn were cash crops. They would sell for money to pay taxes and buy coal.

As soon as the dew was off the grass next morning, Pa went out to cut it with the mowing machine. In the house Ma began to make Mary's velvet hat, and Laura busily knitted a brown silk mitt. At eleven o'clock Ma said, "Mercy, it's time to start dinner already. Run out, Laura, and see if you can find a mess of roasting ears to boil."

The corn was taller than Laura now, a lavish sight to see, with its long leaves rustling thickly and its nodding tasseled tops. As Laura went in between the rows, a great black swirl of birds rose up and whirled above her. The noise of their wings was louder than the rustling of all the long leaves. The birds were so many that they made a shadow like a cloud. It passed swiftly over the corn tops and the crowd of birds settled again.

The ears of corn were plentiful. Nearly every stalk had two ears on it, some had three. The tassels were dry, only a little pollen was still flying and the cornsilks hung like thick, green hair from the tips of the green cornhusks. Here and there a tuft of cornsilk was turning brown, and the ear felt full in the husk when Laura gently pinched it. To make sure, before she tore it from the stalk, she parted the husks to see the rows of milky kernels.

Blackbirds kept flying up around her. Suddenly she stood stock-still. The blackbirds were eating the corn!

Here and there she saw bare tips of ears. The husks were stripped back, and kernels were gone from the cobs. While she stood there, blackbirds settled around her. Their claws clung to the ears, their sharp beaks ripped away the husks, and quickly pecking they swallowed the kernels.

Silently, desperately, Laura ran at them. She felt as if she were screaming. She beat at the birds with her sunbonnet. They rose up swirling on noisy wings and settled again to the corn, before her, behind her, all around her. They swung clinging to the ears, ripping away the husks, swallowing the corn crop. She could do nothing against so many.

She took a few ears in her apron and went to the house. Her heart was beating fast and her wrists and knees trembled. When Ma asked what was the matter, she did not like to answer. "The blackbirds are in the corn," she said. "Oughtn't I to tell Pa?"

"Blackbirds always eat a little corn, I wouldn't worry about it," said Ma. "You might take him a cold drink."

In the hayfield, Pa was not much troubled about the blackbirds. He said he had about cleaned them out of the oats, he had shot a hundred or more. "Likely they'll do some harm to the corn, but that can't be helped," he said.

"There are so many of them," Laura said. "Pa, if you don't get a corn crop, can—can Mary go to college?"

Pa looked bleak. "You think it's as bad as that?"

"There's so many of them," said Laura.

Pa glanced at the sun. "Well, another hour can't make much difference. I'll see about it when I come to dinner."

At noon he took his shotgun to the cornfield. He walked between the corn rows and shot into the cloud of blackbirds as it rose. Every shot brought down a hail of dead birds, but the black cloud settled into the corn again. When he had shot away all his cartridges, the swirl of wings seemed no thinner.

There was not a blackbird in the oatfield. They had left it. But they had eaten every kernel of oats that could be dug out of the shocks. Only straw was left.

Ma thought that she and the girls could keep them away from the corn. They tried to do it. Even Grace ran up and down the rows, screeching and waving her little sunbonnet. The blackbirds only swirled around them and settled again to the ears of corn, tearing the husks and pecking away the kernels.

"You'll wear yourselves out for nothing, Caroline," said Pa. "I'll go to town and buy more cartridges."

When he had gone, Ma said, "Let's see if we can't keep them off till he gets back."

They ran up and down, in the sun and heat, stumbling over the rough sods, screeching and shouting and waving their arms. Sweat ran down their faces and their backs, the sharp cornleaves cut their hands and cheeks. Their throats ached from yelling. And always the swirling wings rose and settled again. Always scores of blackbirds were clinging to the ears, and sharp beaks were tearing and pecking.

At last Ma stopped. "It's no use, girls," she said.

Pa came with more cartridges. All that afternoon he shot blackbirds. They were so thick that every pellet of shot brought down a bird. It seemed that the more he shot, the more there were. It seemed that all the blackbirds in the Territory were hurrying to that feast of corn.

At first there were only common blackbirds. Then came larger, yellow-headed blackbirds, and blackbirds with red heads and a spot of red on each wing. Hundreds of them came.

In the morning a dark spray of blackbirds rose and fell above the cornfield. After breakfast Pa came to the house, bringing both hands full of birds he had shot.

"I never heard of anyone's eating blackbirds," he said, "but these must be good meat, and they're as fat as butter."

"Dress them, Laura, and we'll have them fried for dinner," said Ma. "There's no great loss without some small gain."

Laura dressed the birds, and at noon Ma heated the frying-pan and laid them in it. They fried in their own fat, and at dinner everyone agreed that they were the tenderest, most delicious meat that had ever been on that table.

After dinner, Pa brought another armful of black-birds and an armful of corn.

"We might as well figure that the crop's gone," he said. "This corn's a little too green, but we'd better eat what we can of it before the blackbirds get it all."

"I don't know why I didn't think of it sooner!" Ma exclaimed. "Laura and Carrie, hurry and pick every ear that's possibly old enough to make dried corn. Surely we can save a little, to eat next winter."

Laura knew why Ma had not thought of that sooner; she was too distracted. The corn corp was gone. Pa would have to take from his savings to pay taxes and buy coal. Then how could they manage to send Mary to college this fall?

The blackbirds were so thick now that between the corn rows their wings beat rough against Laura's arms and battered her sunbonnet. She felt sharp little blows on her head, and Carrie cried out that the birds were pecking her. They seemed to feel that the corn was theirs, and to be fighting for it. They rose up harsh at Laura's face and Carrie's, and flew scolding and pecking at their sunbonnets.

Not much corn was left. Even the youngest ears, on which the kernels were hardly more than blisters, had been stripped and pecked at. But Laura and Carrie several times filled their aprons with ears only partly eaten.

When Laura looked for the blackbirds, to dress

them for dinner, she could not find them and Ma would not say where they were.

"Wait and see," Ma answered mysteriously. "Meantime, we'll boil this corn, and cut it off the cobs, to dry."

There is a knack to cutting corn from a cob. The knife must slice evenly, the whole length of the rows, cutting deep enough to get almost the whole kernel, but not so deep as to cut even an edge from the sharp pocket in which each kernel grows. The kernels fall away in milky slabs, moist and sticky.

Ma spread these on a clean, old tablecloth laid outdoors in the sunshine, and she covered them with another cloth, to keep away the blackbirds and the chickens and the flies. The hot sun would dry the corn, and next winter, soaked and boiled, it would be good eating.

"That's an Indian idea," Pa remarked, when he came to dinner. "You'll admit yet, Caroline, there's something to be said for Indians."

"If there is," Ma replied, "you've already said it, many's the time, so I needn't." Ma hated Indians, but now she was brimming with some secret. Laura guessed that it must be the missing blackbirds. "Comb your hair and sit up to the table, Charles," Ma said.

She opened the oven door, and took out the tin milk pan. It was full of something covered thickly over with delicately browned biscuit crust. She set it before Pa and he looked at it amazed. "Chicken pie!"

"'Sing a song of sixpence—'" said Ma.

Laura went on from there, and so did Carrie and Mary and even Grace.

"A pocket full of rye,
    Four and twenty blackbirds,
    Baked in a pie!
    When the pie was opened,
    The birds began to sing.
    Was not that a dainty dish
    To set before the king?"

"Well, I'll be switched!" said Pa. He cut into the pie's crust with a big spoon, and turned over a big chunk of it onto a plate. The underside was steamed and fluffy. Over it he poured spoonfuls of thin brown gravy, and beside it he laid half a blackbird, browned, and so tender that the meat was slipping from the bones. He handed that first plate across the table to Ma.

The scent of that opened pie was making all their mouths water so that they had to swallow again and again while they waited for their portions, and under the table the kitty curved against their legs, her hungry purring running into anxious miows.

"The pan held twelve birds," said Ma. "Just two apiece, but one is all that Grace can possibly eat, so that leaves three for you, Charles."

"It takes you to think up a chicken pie, a year before there's chickens to make it with," Pa said. He ate a mouthful and said, "This beats a chicken pie all hollow."

They all agreed that blackbird pie was even better

than chicken pie. There were, besides, new potatoes and peas, and sliced cucumbers, and young boiled carrots that Ma had thinned from the rows, and creamy cottage cheese. And the day was not even Sunday. As long as the blackbirds lasted, and the garden was green, they could eat like this every day.

Laura thought, "Ma is right, there is always something to be thankful for." Still, her heart was heavy. The oats and the corn crop were gone. She did not know how Mary could go to college now. The beautiful new dress, the two other new dresses, and the pretty underwear, must be laid away until next year. It was a cruel disappointment to Mary.

Pa ate the last spoonful of pink, sugary cream from his saucer of tomatoes, and drank his tea. Dinner was over. He got up and took his hat from its nail and he said to Ma, "Tomorrow's Saturday. If you'll plan to go to town with me, we can pick out Mary's trunk."

Mary gasped. Laura cried out, "Is Mary going to college?"

Pa was astonished. He asked, "What's the matter with you, Laura?"

"How can she?" Laura asked him. "There isn't any corn, or any oats."

"I didn't realize you're old enough to be worrying," said Pa. "I'm going to sell the heifer calf."

Mary cried out, "Oh *no!* Not the heifer!"

In another year the heifer would be a cow. Then

they would have had two cows. Then they would have had milk and butter all the year around. Now, if Pa sold the heifer, they would have to wait two more years for the little calf to grow up.

"Selling her will help out," said Pa. "I ought to get all of fifteen dollars for her."

"Don't worry about it, girls," said Ma. "We must cut our coat to fit the cloth."

"Oh, Pa, it sets you back a whole year," Mary mourned.

"Never mind, Mary," said Pa. "It's time you were going to college, and now we've made up our minds you're going. A flock of pesky blackbirds can't stop us."

MARY GOES TO COLLEGE

The last day came. Tomorrow Mary was going away.

Pa and Ma had brought home her new trunk. It was covered outside with bright tin, pressed into little bumps that made a pattern. Strips of shiny varnished wood were riveted around its middle and up its corners, and three strips ran lengthwise of its curved lid. Short pieces of iron were screwed onto the corners, to protect the wooden strips. When the lid was shut down, two iron tongues fitted into two small iron pockets, and two pairs of iron rings came together so that the trunk could be locked with padlocks.

"It's a good, solid trunk," Pa said. "And I got fifty

feet of stout new rope to rope it with."

Mary's face shone while she felt it over carefully with her sensitive fingers and Laura told her about the bright tin and shiny yellow wood. Ma said, "It is the very newest style in trunks, Mary, and it should last you a lifetime."

Inside, the trunk was smooth-polished wood. Ma lined it carefully with newspapers, and packed tightly into it all Mary's belongings. Every corner she crammed with wadded newspapers, so firmly that nothing could move during the rough journey on the train. She put in many layers of newspapers, too, for she feared that Mary did not have enough clothes to fill the trunk. But when everything was in and cram-jammed down as tightly as possible, the paper-covered mound rose up high enough to fill the curved lid, and Ma sat on it to hold it down while Pa snapped the padlocks.

Then, rolling the trunk end over end, and over and over, Pa tugged and strained loops of the new rope around it, and Laura helped hold the rope tight while he drew the knots fast.

"There," he said finally. "That's one job well done."

As long as they were busy, they could keep pushed deep down inside them the knowledge that Mary was going away. Now everything was done. It was not yet supper time, and the time was empty, for thinking.

Pa cleared his throat and went out of the house. Ma brought her darning basket, but she set it on the table and stood looking out of the window. Grace begged, "Don't go away, Mary, why? Don't go away, tell me a story."

This was the last time that Mary would hold Grace in her lap and tell the story of Grandpa and the panther in the Big Woods of Wisconsin. Grace would be a big girl before Mary came back.

"No, Grace, you must not tease," Ma said, when the story was finished. "What would you like for supper, Mary?" It would be Mary's last supper at home.

"Anything you put on the table is good, Ma," Mary answered.

"It is so hot," Ma said. "I believe I will have cottage cheese balls with onions in them, and the cold creamed peas. Suppose you bring in some lettuce and tomatoes from the garden, Laura."

Suddenly Mary asked, "Could I come with you? I would like a little walk."

"You needn't hurry," Ma told them. "There is plenty of time before supper."

They went walking past the stable and up the low hill beyond. The sun was sinking to rest, like a king, Laura thought, drawing the gorgeous curtains of his great bed around him. But Mary was not pleased by such fancies. So Laura said, "The sun is sinking, Mary, into white downy clouds that spread to the edge of the world. All the tops of them are crimson, and streaming down from the top of the sky are great gorgeous curtains of rose and gold with pearly edges. They are a great canopy over the whole prairie. The little streaks of sky between them are clear, pure green."

Mary stood still. "I'll miss our walks," she said, her voice trembling a little.

"So will I." Laura swallowed, and said, "but only think, you are going to college."

"I couldn't have, without you," Mary said. "You have always helped me to study, and you gave Ma your nine dollars for me."

"It wasn't much," said Laura. "It wasn't anything like I wish I—"

"It was, too!" Mary contradicted. "It was a lot."

Laura's throat choked up. She winked her eyelids hard and took a deep breath but her voice quivered. "I hope you like college, Mary."

"Oh, I will. I will!" Mary breathed. "Think of being able to study and learn—Oh, everything! Even to play the organ. I do owe it partly to you, Laura. Even if you aren't teaching school yet, you have helped me to go."

"I am going to teach school as soon as I am old enough," said Laura. "Then I can help more."

"I wish you didn't have to," Mary said.

"Well, I do have to," Laura replied. "But I can't, till

I'm sixteen. That's the law, a teacher has to be sixteen years old."

"I won't be here then," said Mary. Then suddenly they felt as if she were going away forever. The years ahead of them were empty and frightening.

"Oh, Laura, I never have been away from home before. I don't know what I'll do," Mary confessed. She was trembling all over.

"It will be all right," Laura told her stoutly. "Ma and Pa are going with you, and I know you can pass the examinations. Don't be scared."

"I'm not scared. I won't *be* scared," Mary insisted. "I'll be lonesome. But that can't be helped."

"No," Laura said. After a minute she cleared her throat and told Mary, "The sun has gone through the white clouds. It is a huge, pulsing ball of liquid fire. The clouds above it are scarlet and crimson and gold and purple, and the great sweeps of cloud over the whole sky are burning flames."

"It seems to me I can feel their light on my face," Mary said. "I wonder if the sky and the sunsets are different in Iowa?"

Laura did not know. They came slowly down the low hill. This was the end of their last walk together, or at least, their last walk for such a long time that it seemed forever.

"I am sure I can pass the examinations, because you helped me so much," Mary said. "You went over every word of your lessons with me, until I do know everything in the school books. But Laura, what will you do? Pa is spending so much for me—the trunk, and a new coat, a new pair of shoes, the railroad fares, and all—it worries me. How can he ever manage school books and clothes for you and Carrie?"

"Never mind, Pa and Ma will manage," said Laura. "You know they always do."

Early next morning, even before Laura was dressed, Ma was scalding and plucking the blackbirds that Pa had killed. She fried them after breakfast, and as soon as they were cool she packed in a shoe box the lunch to take on the train.

Pa and Ma and Mary had bathed the night before. Now Mary put on her best old calico dress and her second-best shoes. Ma dressed in her summer challis, and Pa put on his Sunday suit. A neighbor boy had agreed to drive them to the depot. Pa and Ma would be gone a week, and when they came home without Mary they could walk from town.

The wagon came. The freckled boy, with red hair sticking through a rent in his straw hat, helped Pa load Mary's trunk into the wagon. The sun was shining hot and the wind was blowing.

"Now, Carrie and Grace, be good girls and mind Laura," Ma said. "Remember to keep the chickens' water pan filled, Laura, and look out for hawks, and scald and sun the milk pans every day."

113

"Yes, Ma," they all answered.

"Good-by," Mary said. "Good-by Laura. And Carrie. And Grace."

"Good-by," Laura and Carrie managed to say. Grace only stared round-eyed. Pa helped Mary to climb up the wagonwheel to sit with Ma and the boy on the wagon seat. He took his seat on the trunk.

"All right, let's go," he said to the boy. "Good-by, girls."

The wagon started. Grace's mouth opened wide and she bawled.

"For shame, Grace! For *shame!* a big girl like you, *crying!*" Laura choked out. Her throat was swelling so that it hurt. Carrie looked as though she might cry in a moment. "*Shame* on you!" Laura said again, and Grace gulped down a last sob.

Pa and Ma and Mary did not look back. They had to go. The wagon taking them away left silence behind it. Laura had never felt such a stillness. It was not the happy stillness of the prairie. She felt it in the very pit of her stomach.

"Come," she said. "We'll go into the house."

That silence had settled into the house. It was so still that Laura felt she must whisper. Grace smothered a whimpering. They stood there in their own house and felt nothing around them but silence and emptiness. Mary was gone.

Grace began to cry again and two large tears stood

in Carrie's eyes. This would never do. Right now, and for a whole week, everything was in Laura's charge, and Ma must be able to depend on her.

"Listen to me, Carrie and Grace," she said briskly. "We are going to clean this house from top to bottom, and we'll begin right now! So when Ma comes home, she'll find the fall housecleaning done."

There had never been such a busy time in all Laura's life. The work was hard, too. She had not realized how heavy a quilt is, to lift soaked and dripping from a tub, and to wring out, and to hang on a line. She had not known how hard it would be, sometimes, never to be cross with Grace who was always trying to help and only making more work. It was amazing, too, how dirty they all got, while cleaning a house that had seemed quite clean. The harder they worked, the dirtier everything became.

The worst day of all was very hot. They had tugged and lugged the straw ticks outdoors, and emptied them and washed them, and when they were dry they had filled them with sweet fresh hay. They had got the bed springs off the bedsteads and leaned them against the walls, and Laura had jammed her finger. Now they were pulling the bedsteads apart. Laura jerked at one corner and Carrie jerked at the other. The corners came apart, and suddenly the headboard came down on Laura's head so that she saw stars.

"Oh, Laura! did it hurt you?" Carrie cried.

"Well, not very much," Laura said. She pushed the headboard against the wall, and it slid down softly and hit her anklebone. "Ouch!" she couldn't help yelling. Then she added, "Let it lie there if it wants to!"

"We have to scrub the floor," Carrie pointed out.

"I know we have to," Laura said grimly. She sat on the floor, gripping her ankle. Her straggling hair stuck to her sweating neck. Her dress was damp and hot and dirty, and her fingernails were positively black. Carrie's face was smudged with dust and sweat and there were bits of hay in her hair.

"We ought to have a bath," Laura murmured. Suddenly she cried out, *"Where's Grace?"*

They had not thought of Grace for some time. Grace had once been lost on the prairie. Two children at Brookins, lost on the prairie, had died before they could be found.

"Here I yam," Grace answered sweetly, coming in. "It's raining."

"No!" Laura exclaimed. Indeed, a shadow was over the house. A few large drops were falling. At that moment, thunder crashed. Laura screamed, "Carrie! The straw ticks! The bedding!"

They ran. The straw ticks were not very heavy, but they were stuffed fat with hay. They were hard to hold on to. The edge kept slipping out of Laura's grasp or Carrie's. When they got one to the house, they had to hold it up edgewise to get it through the doorway.

"We can hold it up or we can move it, we can't do both," Carried panted. Already the swift thunderstorm was rolling overhead and rain was falling fast.

"Get out of the way!" Laura shouted. Somehow she pushed and carried the whole straw tick into the house. It was too late to bring in the other one, or the bedding from the line. Rain was pouring down.

The bedding would dry on the line, but the other straw tick must be emptied again, washed again, and filled again. Straw ticks must be perfectly dry, or the hay in them would smell musty.

"We can move everything out of the other bedroom into the front room, and go on scrubbing," said Laura. So they did that. For some time there was no sound but thunder and beating rain, and the swish of scrubbing cloths and the wringing out. Laura and Carrie had worked backward on hands and knees almost across the bedroom floor, when Grace called happily, "I'm helping!"

She was standing on a chair and blacking the stove. She was splashed from head to foot with blacking. On the floor all around the stove were dribbles and splotches of blacking. Grace had filled the blacking box full of water. As she looked up beaming for Laura's approval, she gave the smeared stove top another swipe of the blacking cloth, and pushed the box of soft blacking off it.

Her blue eyes were filled with tears.

Laura gave one wild look at that house that Ma had left so neat and pretty. She just managed to say, "Never mind, Grace; don't cry. I'll clean it up." Then she sank down on the stacked pieces of the bedsteads and let her forehead sink to her pulled-up knees.

"Oh, Carrie, I just don't seem to know how to manage the way Ma does!" she almost wailed.

That was the worst day. On Friday the house was almost in order, and they worried lest Ma come home too soon. They worked fair into the night that night, and on Saturday it was almost midnight before Laura and Carrie took their baths and collapsed to sleep. But for Sunday the house was immaculate.

The floor around the stove was scrubbed bone-white. Only faintest traces of the blacking remained. The beds were made up with clean, bright quilts and they smelled sweetly of fresh hay. The windowpanes glittered. Every shelf in the cupboards was scrubbed and every dish washed. "And we'll eat bread and drink milk from now on, and *keep* the dishes clean!" said Laura.

There remained only the curtains to be washed and ironed and hung, and of course the usual washing to do, on Monday. They were glad that Sunday is a day of rest.

Early Monday morning, Laura washed the curtains. They were dry when she and Carrie hung the rest of the washing on the line. They sprinkled the curtains and ironed them, and hung them at the window. The house was perfect.

"We'll keep Grace out of it till Pa and Ma come home," Laura said privately to Carrie. Neither of them felt like even taking a walk. So they sat on the grass in the shade of the house and watched Grace run about, and watched for the smoke of the train.

They saw it rolling up from the prairie and fading slowly along the skyline like a line of writing that they could not read. They heard the train whistle. After a pause it whistled again, and the curling smoke began again to write low above the skyline. They had almost decided that Pa and Ma had not come yet, when they saw them small and far away, walking out on the road from town.

Then all the lonesomeness for Mary came back, as sharply as if she had just gone away.

They met Pa and Ma at the edge of Big Slough, and for a little while they all talked at once.

Pa and Ma were greatly pleased with the college. They said it was a fine place, a large brick building. Mary would be warm and comfortable in it when winter came. She would have good food, and she was with a crowd of pleasant girls. Ma liked her roommate very much. The teachers were kind. Mary had passed the examinations with flying colors. Ma had seen no clothes there nicer than hers. She was going to study political economy, and literature, and higher mathematics, and sewing, knitting, beadwork, and music. The college had a parlor organ.

Laura was so glad for Mary that she could almost forget the lonesome ache of missing her. Mary had always so loved to study. Now she could revel in studying so much that she had never before had a chance to learn.

"Oh, she must stay there, she *must*," Laura thought, and she renewed her vow to study hard, though she didn't like to, and get a teacher's certificate as soon as she was sixteen, so that she could earn the money to keep Mary in college.

She had forgotten that week of housecleaning, but as they came to the house Ma asked, "Carrie, what are you and Grace smiling about? You're keeping something up your sleeves!"

Then Grace jumped up and down and shouted, "I blacked the stove!"

"So you did," said Ma, going into the house. "It looks very nice, but Grace, I am sure that Laura helped you black it. You must not say—" Then she saw the curtains. "Why, Laura," she said, "did you wash the—and the windows—and— Why, I declare!"

"We did the fall housecleaning for you, Ma," said Laura, and Carrie chimed in, "We washed the bedding, and filled the straw ticks, and scrubbed the floors, and everything."

Ma lifted her hands in surprise, then she sat weakly down and let her hands fall. "My goodness!"

Next day, when she unpacked her valise, she surprised them. She came from the bedroom with three small flat packages, and gave one to Laura, one to Carrie, and one to Grace.

In Grace's package was a picture book. The colorful pictures, on shiny paper, were pasted to cloth leaves of many pretty colors, and every leaf was pinked around its edges.

In Laura's package was a beautiful small book, too. It was thin, and wider than it was tall. On its red cover, embossed in gold, were the words,

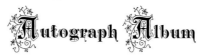

The pages, of different soft colors, were blank. Carrie had another exactly like it, except that the cover of hers was blue and gold.

"I found that autograph albums are all the fashion nowadays," said Ma. "All the most fashionable girls in Vinton have them."

"What are they, exactly?" Laura asked.

"You ask a friend to write a verse on one of the blank pages and sign her name to it," Ma explained. "If she has an autograph album, you do the same for her, and you keep the albums to remember each other by."

"I won't mind going to school so much now," said

Carrie. "I will show my autograph album to all the strange girls, and if they are nice to me I will let them write in it."

Ma was glad that the autograph albums pleased them both. She said, "Your Pa and I wanted our other girls to have something from Vinton, Iowa, where Mary is going to college."

MISS WILDER
TEACHES SCHOOL

arly on the First Day of School Laura and
Carrie set out. They wore their best sprigged
calico dresses, for Ma said they would out-
grow them before next summer, anyway. They carried their school books under their arms, and Laura
carried their tin dinner pail.

The coolness of night still lingered in the early sunlight. Under the high blue sky the green of the prairie
was fading to soft brown and mauve. A little wind
wandered over it carrying the fragrance of ripening

124

grasses and the pungent smell of wild sunflowers. All along the road the yellow blossoms were nodding, and in its grassy middle they struck with soft thumps against the swinging dinner pail. Laura walked in one wheel track, and Carrie in the other.

"Oh, I do hope Miss Wilder will be a good teacher," said Carrie. "Do you think so?"

"Pa must think so, he's on the school board," Laura pointed out. "Though maybe they hired her because she's the Wilder boy's sister. Oh, Carrie, remember those beautiful brown horses?"

"Just because he has those horses don't make his sister nice," Carrie argued. "But maybe she is."

"Anyway, she knows how to teach. She has a certificate," said Laura. She sighed, thinking how hard she must study to get her own certificate.

Main Street was growing longer. Now a new livery stable was on Pa's side of it, across from the bank. A new grain elevator stood tall beyond the far end of the street, across from the railroad tracks.

"Why are all those lots vacant, between the livery stable and Pa's?" Carrie wondered.

Laura did not know. Anyway, she liked the wild prairie grasses there. Pa's new haystacks stood thick around his barn. He would not have to haul hay from the claim to burn this winter.

She and Carrie turned west on Second Street. Beyond the schoolhouse, new little claim shanties were scattered now. A new flour mill was racketing by the railroad tracks, and across the vacant lots between Second Street and Third Street could be seen the skeleton of the new church building on Third Street. Men were working on it. A great many strangers were in the crowd of pupils gathered near the schoolhouse door.

Carrie timidly shrank back, and Laura's knees weakened, but she must be brave for Carrie, so she went on boldly. The palms of her hands grew moist with sweat when so many eyes looked at her. There must have been twenty boys and girls.

Taking firm grip on her courage, Laura walked up to them and Carrie went with her. The boys stood back a little on one side and the girls on the other. It seemed to Laura that she simply could not walk to the schoolhouse steps.

Then suddenly she saw on the steps Mary Power and Minnie Johnson. She knew them; they had been in school last fall, before the blizzards came. Mary Power said, "Hello, Laura Ingalls!"

Her dark eyes were glad to see Laura, and so was Minnie Johnson's freckled face. Laura felt all right then. She felt she would always be very fond of Mary Power.

"We've picked out our seats, we're going to sit together," said Minnie. "But why don't you sit across the aisle from us?"

They went into the schoolhouse together. Mary's books and Minnie's were on the back desk next to the wall, on the girls' side. Laura laid hers on the desk across the aisle. Those two back seats were the very best seats. Carrie, of course, must sit nearer the teacher, with the smaller girls.

Miss Wilder was coming down the aisle, with the school bell in her hand. Her hair was dark and her eyes were gray. She seemed a very pleasant person. Her dark gray dress was stylishly made, like Mary's best one, tight and straight in the front, with a pleated ruffle just touching the floor, and an overskirt draped and puffed above a little train.

"You girls have chosen your seats, haven't you?" she said pleasantly.

"Yes, ma'am," Minnie Johnson said bashfully, but Mary Power smiled and said, "I am Mary Power, and this is Minnie Johnson, and Laura Ingalls. We would like to keep these seats if we may, please. We are the biggest girls in school."

"Yes, you may keep these seats," said Miss Wilder, very pleasantly.

She went to the door and rang the bell. Pupils came crowding in, till nearly all the seats were filled. On the girls' side, only one seat was left vacant. On the boys' side, all the back seats were empty because the big boys would not come to school until the winter term. They were still working on the claims now.

Laura saw that Carrie was sitting happily with Mamie Beardsley, near the front where younger girls should sit. Then suddenly she saw a strange girl hesitating in the aisle. She seemed about as old as Laura, and as shy. She was small and slim. Her soft brown eyes were large in a small round face. Her hair was black and softly wavy, and around her forehead the short hairs curled. She was flushing pink from nervousness. Timidly she glanced at Laura.

Unless Laura would take her as a seatmate, she must sit alone in the empty seat.

Quickly Laura smiled, and patted the seat beside her. The new girl's great brown eyes laughed joyously. She laid her books on the desk and sat down beside Laura.

When Miss Wilder had called the school to order, she took the record book and went from desk to desk, writing down the pupils' names. Laura's seatmate answered that her name was Ida Wright, but she was called Ida Brown. She was the adopted daughter of Reverend Brown and Mrs. Brown.

Rev. Brown was the new Congregational minister who had just come to town. Laura knew that Pa and Ma did not like him very much, but she was sure she liked Ida.

Miss Wilder had put the record book in her desk and was ready to begin school, when the door opened again. Everyone looked to see who had come tardily to school on this First Day.

Laura could not believe her eyes. The girl who came in was Nellie Oleson, from Plum Creek in Minnesota.

She had grown taller than Laura, and she was much slimmer. She was willowy, while Laura was still as round and dumpy as a little French horse. But Laura knew her at once, though it was two years since she had seen her. Nellie's nose was still held high and sniffing, her small eyes were still set close to it, and her mouth was prim and prissy.

Nellie was the girl who had made fun of Laura and Mary because they were only country girls, while her father was a storekeeper. She had spoken impudently to Ma. She had been mean to Jack, the good and faithful bulldog, who was dead now.

She had come late to school, yet she stood looking as if the school were not good enough for her. She wore a fawn-colored dress made with a polonaise. Deep pleated ruffles were around the bottom of the skirt, around her neck, and falling from the edges of the wide sleeves. At her throat was a full jabot of lace. Her fair, straight hair was drawn smoothly back from her sharp face, and twisted into a tall French knot. She held her head high and looked scornfully down her nose.

"I would like a back seat, if you please," she said to Miss Wilder. And she gave Laura a nudging look that said, "Get out and give me that seat."

Laura sat more solidly and firmly where she was, and looked back at Nellie through narrowed eyes.

Everyone else looked at Miss Wilder to see what she would do. Miss Wilder cleared her throat nervously. Laura kept on looking at Nellie, till Nellie looked away. She looked at Minnie Johnson, and said, nodding toward Minnie's seat, "That place will do."

"Will you change, Minnie?" Miss Wilder asked. But she had promised that Minnie might sit there.

Slowly Minnie answered, "Yes, ma'am." Slowly she picked up her books and went forward to the vacant seat. Mary Power did not move, and Nellie stood waiting in the aisle; she would not go around the seat to the place that Minnie had left.

"Now, Mary," Miss Wilder said, "if you will move over and make room for our new girl, we will all be settled."

Mary stood up. "I'll go with Minnie," she said shortly. "I'd rather."

Nellie sat down smiling. She had the best seat in the room, and the whole desk for her own use.

Laura was meanly glad to hear her tell Miss Wilder, for the record book, that her father was living on a claim north of town. So Nellie herself was a country girl now! Then suddenly Laura realized that Pa was moving to town for the winter; she and Carrie would be town girls.

Miss Wilder rapped the desk with her ruler, and said, "Attention, boys and girls!" Then she made a little speech, smiling all the time.

She said, "Now we are all ready to begin the school term, and we're all going to do our best to make it a

success, aren't we? You know you are all here to learn as much as you possibly can, and I am here to help you. You must not look upon me as a taskmistress, but as a friend. We are all going to be the very best of friends, I'm sure."

The small boys were squirming, and Laura wanted to. She could not look at Miss Wilder's smiling any more.

She only wished that Miss Wilder would stop talking. But Miss Wilder went on in her smiling voice: "None of us will ever be unkind or selfish, will we? I am sure that not one of you will ever be unruly, so there need be no thought of punishments here in our happy school. We shall all be friends together and love and help each other."

Then at last she said, "You may take your books." There were no recitations that morning, for Miss Wilder was sorting the pupils into their classes. Laura and Ida, Mary Power and Minnie, and Nellie Oleson, were the only big girls. They were the most advanced class, and the whole class until the big boys would come to school.

At recess they stayed in a group, getting acquainted. Ida was as warm and friendly as she looked. "I'm only an adopted child," she said. "Mother Brown took me out of a Home, but she must have liked me to do that, don't you think so?"

"Of course she liked you, she couldn't have helped

it," Laura said. She could imagine what a pretty baby Ida must have been, with her black curls and big, laughing brown eyes.

But Nellie wanted all attention for herself.

"I really don't know whether we'll like it out here," Nellie said. "We are from the East. We are not used to such a rough country and rough people."

"You come from western Minnesota, from the same place we did," said Laura.

"Oh, *that!*" Nellie brushed away Minnesota with her hand. "We were there only a little while. We come from the East, from New York State."

"We all come from the East," Mary Power told her shortly. "Come on, let's all go outdoors in the sunshine."

"My goodness, no!" said Nellie. "Why, this wind will tan your skin!"

They were all tanned but Nellie, and she went on airily, "I may have to live out in this rough country for a little while, but I shan't let it spoil my complexion. In the East, a lady always keeps her skin white and her hands smooth." Nellie's hands were white and slender.

There was no time to go outdoors, anyway. Recess was over. Miss Wilder went to the door and rang the bell.

At home that night, Carrie chattered about the day at school until Pa said she was as talkative as a bluejay.

"Let Laura get a word in edgewise. Why are you so quiet, Laura? Anything go wrong?"

Then Laura told about Nellie Oleson and all she had said and done. She finished, "Miss Wilder shouldn't have let her take the seat away from Mary Power and Minnie."

"Nor should you ever criticize a teacher, Laura," Ma gently reminded her.

Laura felt her cheeks grow hot. She knew what a great opportunity it was, to go to school. Miss Wilder was there to help her learn, she should be grateful, she should never impertinently criticize. She should only try to be perfect in her lessons and in deportment. Yet she could not help thinking, "Just the same, she shouldn't have! It was not fair."

"So the Olesons came from New York State, did they?" Pa was amused. "That's not so much to brag about."

Laura remembered then that Pa had lived in New York State when he was a boy.

He went on, "I don't know how it happened, but Oleson lost everything he had in Minnesota. He hasn't a thing in the world now but his homestead claim, and they tell me his folks back East are helping him out, or he couldn't hang on to that till he makes a crop. Maybe Nellie feels she's got to brag a little, to hold her own. I wouldn't let it worry me, Laura."

"But she had such pretty clothes," Laura protested. "And she can't do a bit of work, she keeps her face and her hands so white."

"You could wear your sunbonnet, you know," said Ma. "As for her pretty dresses, likely they come out of a barrel, and maybe she's like the girl in the song, who was so fine 'with a double ruffle around her neck and nary a shoe to wear.'"

Laura supposed she should be sorry for Nellie, but she wasn't. She wished that Nellie Oleson had stayed in Plum Creek.

Pa got up from the supper table and drew his chair near the open door. He said, "Bring me the fiddle, Laura. I want to try a song I heard a fellow singing the other day. He whistled the chorus. I believe the fiddle will beat his whistling."

Softly Laura and Carrie washed the dishes, not to miss a note of the music. Pa sang, low and longingly, with the sweet clear voice of the fiddle.

> "Then meet me—Oh, meet me,
>   When you hear
>   The first whip-poor-will call—"

"Whip-poor-will," the fiddle called, and fluting, throbbing like the throat of the bird, "Whip-poor-will," the fiddle answered. Near and pleading, "Whip-poor-will," then far and soft but coming nearer, "Whip-poor-will," till all the gathering twilight was filled with the wooing of the birds.

Laura's thoughts untangled from their ugly snarls and became smooth and peaceful. She thought, "I will be good. It doesn't matter how hateful Nellie Oleson is, I will be good."

SNUG FOR WINTER

All through the pleasant fall weather Laura and Carrie were busy girls. In the mornings they helped do the chores and get breakfast. Then they filled their dinner pail, dressed for school and hurried away on the mile walk to town. After school they hurried home, for there was work to do until darkness came.

Saturday was a whole day of busy working, in a hurry to be ready to move to town.

Laura and Carrie picked up potatoes while Pa dug them. They cut the tops from turnips and helped Pa pile them in the wagon. They pulled and topped the carrots, too, and the beets and onions. They gathered the tomatoes and the ground-cherries.

The ground-cherries grew on low leafy bushes. Thick on the stems under the large leaves hung the six-cornered bells, pale grey and thinner than paper, and inside each bell was a plump, golden, juicy round fruit.

The husk-tomatoes were covered with a smooth, dull-brown husk. When this was opened there lay the round, bright-purple tomato, larger than a ground-cherry but much smaller than the red tomatoes that openly flaunted their bright colors.

All day long while the girls were in school, Ma made preserves of the red tomatoes, of the purple husk-tomatoes, and of the golden ground-cherries. She made pickles of the green tomatoes that would not have time to ripen before it froze. The house was full of the sirupy scent of preserves and the spicy odor of pickles.

"We will take our provisions with us when we move to town this time," said Pa with satisfaction. "And we must go soon. I don't want another October blizzard to catch us in this thin-walled little house."

"This winter isn't going to be as hard as last winter," Laura said. "The weather doesn't feel the same."

"No," Pa agreed. "It isn't likely this winter will be as hard, nor come as soon, but this time I intend to be ready for it when it does come."

He hauled the oat straw and the corn fodder and

stacked them near his haystacks in town. He hauled the potatoes and turnips, beets and carrots, and stored them in the cellar of his store building. Then busily all one Monday evening and far into the night, Laura and Carrie helped Ma pack clothes and dishes and books.

It was then that Laura discovered a secret. She was on her knees, lifting winter underwear out of Ma's

bottom bureau drawer, and under the red flannels she felt something hard. She put in her hand and drew out a book.

It was a perfectly new book, beautifully bound in green cloth with a gilded pattern pressed into it. The smooth, straight, gilt edges of the pages looked like solid gold. On the cover two curving scrolls of lovely, fancy letters made the words,

Laura was so startled and so amazed by this rich and beautiful book, hidden there among the flannels, that she almost dropped it. It fell open on her hands. In the lamplight the fresh, untouched pages lay spread, each exciting with unread words printed upon it in clear, fine type. Straight, thin red lines enclosed each oblong of printing, like the treasure it was, and outside the red lines were the page's pure margins.

Near the bottom of the left-hand page was a short line in larger type: THE LOTOS-EATERS.

"Courage!" was the first word under that, and breathlessly Laura read,

> "Courage!" he said, and pointed to the land,
> "This mounting wave will roll us shoreward soon."
> In the afternoon they came unto a land
> In which it seemed always afternoon.

All round the coast the languid air did swoon,
Breathing like one that hath a weary dream.
Full-faced above the valley stood the moon;
And, like a—

Laura stopped, aghast. Suddenly she had realized what she was doing. Ma must have hidden this book. Laura had no right to read it. Quickly she shut her eyes, and then she shut the book. It was almost more than she could do, not to read just one word more, just to the end of that one line. But she knew that she must not yield one tiny bit of temptation.

She put the book where it had been, between the red flannels. She put the flannels back into the drawer, shut the drawer, and opened the drawer above it. Then she did not know what to do.

She should confess to Ma what she had done. But instantly she knew that Ma must be keeping the book hidden, for a surprise. She thought swiftly, and her heart was pounding hard, that Pa and Ma must have bought that book in Vinton, Iowa; they must be saving it for a Christmas present. A book so rich and fine, a book of poems, could only be a Christmas present. And Laura was the oldest girl at home now; it must be a Christmas present for her!

If she confessed to Ma, she would spoil their Christmas pleasure, that they were looking forward to. Pa and Ma would be so disappointed.

It seemed a long time since she had found that book, but really it had only been a moment. Ma came in hurriedly and said, "I'll finish in here, Laura, you go to bed now, it's past your bedtime."

"Yes, Ma," Laura said. She knew that Ma had feared she would open that lower drawer and find the book. Never before had she kept a guilty secret from Ma, but now she did not say a word.

After school next day, she and Carrie did not take the long walk to the claim. Instead they stopped at Pa's store building at the corner of Second Street and Main. Pa and Ma had moved into town for the winter.

The stove and the cupboard were set up in the kitchen. Upstairs the bedsteads stood under the slanting shingle roof, the straw ticks lay plumply on them under heaped quilts and pillows. Making the beds was all that Ma had left for Laura and Carrie to do. And Laura was sure that the Christmas book, Tennyson's Poems, was hidden in Ma's bureau drawer. She would never look to see, of course.

Yet every time she saw the bureau she could not help thinking,

> Full-faced above the valley stood the moon;
> And, like a—

Like what? She would have to wait until Christmas to learn the rest of that lovely poem. "Courage!" he said, and pointed to the land. "This mounting wave will roll us shoreward soon." In the afternoon they came unto a land in which it seemed always afternoon. But it did not seem to Laura that Christmas was soon.

Downstairs Ma had already made the big storeroom neat and pleasant. The heater was polished, the curtains hung fresh at the window, the clean little rag rugs lay on the swept floor. The two rocking chairs were in the sunny corner. Mary's was empty.

Often Laura missed Mary so much that she ached. But it would do no good to speak of it. Mary was in college, where she had so wanted to be. A teacher had written Pa that she was well and making rapid progress; soon she would be able to write a letter.

So no one spoke of the emptiness they all felt now. Quietly and cheerfully they went about getting supper and setting the table, and Ma did not know that she sighed when she said, "Well, we are all settled snug for the winter."

"Yes," Pa said. "This time we are well fixed for it."

They were not the only ones who were ready. Everyone in the town had been preparing. The lumberyard was stocked with coal, the merchants had stuffed their stores full of goods. There was flour at the mill, and wheat in its bins.

"We will have coal to burn and something to eat all winter, if the trains can't get through," Pa gloated. It was good to feel safe and prospering, with food enough and fuel enough so that they need not dread hunger or cold.

Laura missed the pleasant long walks to school and back. She had delighted in them. But now there was no hurry in the mornings, since she had no chores to do. Pa did them all, now that he had no farm work. And the shorter walk was better for Carrie.

Pa and Ma and Laura were worried about Carrie. She had never been strong, and she was not recovering from the hard winter as she should. They spared her all but the lightest housework, and Ma coaxed her appetite with the best there was to eat. Still she was thin and pale, small for her age and spindly. Her eyes were too large in her peaked little face. Often in the mornings, though the walk was only a mile and Laura carried her books, Carrie grew tired before they reached the schoolhouse. Sometimes her head ached so badly that she failed in her recitations. Living in town was easier. It would be much better for Carrie.

SCHOOL DAYS

Laura was enjoying school. She knew all the pupils now, and she and Ida, Mary Power and Minnie, were becoming fast friends. At recess and noon they were always together.

In the crisp, sunny weather the boys played ante-over and catch, and sometimes they just threw the ball against the schoolhouse and ran jostling and bumping together to catch it in the wild prairie grasses. Often they coaxed Laura, "Come, play with us, Laura. Aw, come on!"

It was tomboyish to run and play, at her age. But she did so love to run and jump and catch the ball and throw it, that sometimes she did join in the games. The boys were only little boys. She liked them, and she never complained when the games grew rough now and then. One day she overheard Charley saying, "She isn't a sissy, even if she is a girl."

Hearing that made her feel glad and cozy. When even little boys like a big girl, she knows that everyone likes her.

The other girls knew that Laura was not really a tomboy, even when her face was hot from running and jumping, and the hairpins were coming loose in her hair. Ida sometimes played, too, and Mary Power and Minnie would look on, applauding. Only Nellie Oleson turned up her nose.

Nellie would not even go walking, though they asked her politely. It was all "too rough, really," she said.

"She's afraid of spoiling her New York State complexion," Ida laughed.

"I think she stays in the school house to make friends with Miss Wilder," said Mary Power. "She talks to her all the time."

"Well, let her. We have a much better time without her," Minnie said.

"Miss Wilder used to live in New York State, too. Likely that is what they talk about," Laura remarked.

Mary Power gave her a laughing, sidelong glance and squeezed her arm. No one called Nellie "teacher's pet," but that was what they were thinking. Laura did not care. She was at the head of the class in all their studies, and she need not be a teacher's pet to stay there.

Every evening after supper she studied till bedtime. It was then that she missed Mary most painfully. They had always gone over their lessons together. But she knew that far away in Iowa, Mary was studying, too, and if she were to stay in college and enjoy all its wonderful opportunities of learning, Laura must get a teacher's certificate.

All this went through her head in a flash, while she went walking, arm in arm with Mary Power and Ida.

"You know what I think?" Minnie asked.

"No, what?" they all asked her.

"I bet that's what Nellie's scheming about," Minnie said, and she nodded at a team that was coming toward them along the wagon tracks ahead. It was the brown Morgan horses.

All their slender legs were moving swiftly, their hoofs raising little explosions of dust. Their glossy shoulders glistened, their black manes and tails blew shining in the wind. Their ears pricked forward, and their glancing bright eyes saw everything gaily. Dancing little red tassels trimmed their bridles.

Sunlight ran glistening on the curve of their arched necks, straight along their smooth sides and curving again on their round haunches. And behind them ran a shining new buggy. Its dashboard glittered, its spotless black top curved over the seat on gleaming black spokes, its wheels were red. Laura had never seen such a buggy.

"Why didn't you bow, Laura?" Ida asked when it had sped by.

"Didn't you see him raise his hat to us?" said Mary Power. Laura had seen only the beautiful horses, till the buggy flashed before her eyes.

"Oh, I'm sorry. I didn't mean to be impolite," she said. "They are just like poetry, aren't they?"

"You don't mean she's setting her cap for him, Minnie," Mary Power said. "Why, he's a grown-up man, he's a homesteader."

"I've seen her looking at those horses," said Minnie. "I bet she's made up her mind to get a ride behind them. You know that kind of scheming look she has sometimes. And now that he's got such a buggy—"

"He didn't have any buggy last Fourth of July," said Laura.

"It's just come from the east," Minnie told them. "He ordered it after he sold his wheat crop. He had a wonderful wheat crop." Minnie always knew such news, because her brother Arthur told her.

Slowly Mary Power said, "I do believe you are right, I wouldn't put it past her."

Laura felt a little guilty. She wouldn't make up to Miss Wilder just to get a ride behind Almanzo Wilder's horses. Yet she had often thought that if Miss

Wilder liked her, she might someday take her riding behind them.

Miss Wilder had taken a claim on this road, only a quarter of a mile beyond the schoolhouse. She lived there in a little claim shanty. Almanzo often brought her to the schoolhouse in the morning, or stopped after school to take her home. And always, when she saw those horses, Laura hoped that Miss Wilder might, perhaps, sometime, ask her for a ride. Could it be that she was as horrid as Nellie Oleson?

Now that she had seen that buggy, more than ever Laura wanted such a ride. How could she prevent such thoughts, when those horses were so beautiful and the buggy so swift?

"It's almost time for the bell," Ida said, and they all turned back to the schoolhouse. They must not be late. In the entry they drank from the dipper that floated in the water pail there. Then they went in, tanned and windblown, and hot and dusty. Nellie was neat and ladylike, her skin was white, and every hair of her head was in its place.

She looked down her nose at them, and smiled a lofty smile. Laura looked straight back at her, and Nellie gave a little flounce of her shoulder and chin.

"You needn't think you're so much, Laura Ingalls!" Nellie said. "Miss Wilder says your father has nothing much to say about this school, even if he is on the school board."

149

"Why!" Laura gasped.

"I guess he's got as much to say about this school as anybody, and maybe more!" Ida said stoutly. "Hasn't he, Laura?"

"He certainly has!" Laura cried.

"Yes," said Mary Power. "He has more, because Laura and Carrie are in this school and the others on the board haven't any children."

Laura was furious with rage, that Nellie dared to say anything against Pa. On the steps Miss Wilder was ringing the bell and its noise clanged in Laura's head. She said, "It's just too bad your folks are nothing but country folks, Nellie. If you lived in town, then maybe your father could be on the school board and have something to say about this school."

Nellie was going to slap her. Laura saw her hand rising, and she barely had time to think that she must not, *must not* slap Nellie, and to hope she wouldn't. Then Nellie's hand dropped quickly and she slid into her seat. Miss Wilder had come in.

All the pupils came clattering, and Laura sat down in her own seat. She was still so angry that she could hardly see. Under the desk-top Ida's hand gave her clenched fist a quick little squeeze that meant, "Good for you! You served her right!"

SENT HOME
FROM SCHOOL

Miss Wilder was puzzling everyone in school. From the first day, of course, the boys had been trying to find out how far they could go in naughtiness before she made them behave themselves, and no one could understand why she did not show them.

At first they fidgeted and then they began making little noises with their books and slates. Miss Wilder paid no attention until the noise was disturbing. Then she did not speak sharply to the noisiest boy, but smiled at them all and politely asked them to be quieter.

"I know you do not realize that you are disturbing others," she said.

They did not know what to make of this. When she turned to the blackboard, the noise would grow loud again. The boys even began to whisper.

Every day Miss Wilder asked everyone, several times, to be just a little quieter, please. This was not fair to those who were making no noise at all. Soon all the boys were whispering, nudging each other, and sometimes slyly scuffing in their seats. Some of the little girls wrote notes to each other on their slates.

Still Miss Wilder did not punish anyone. One afternoon she rapped on her desk to call the whole school to attention, and talked to them about how good she was sure they all meant to be. She said she did not believe in punishing children. She meant to rule them by love, not fear. She liked them all and she was sure that they liked her. Even the big girls were embarrassed by her way of talking.

"Birds in their little nests agree," she said, smiling, and Laura and Ida almost squirmed from embarrassment. Besides, that showed that she knew nothing at all about birds.

Miss Wilder kept on always smiling even when her eyes were worried. Only her smiles at Nellie Oleson seemed real. She seemed to feel that she could depend on Nellie Oleson.

"She's a—well, almost a hypocrite," Minnie said, low, one day at recess. They were standing at the window, watching the boys play ball. Miss Wilder and Nellie were chatting together by the stove. It was cooler at the window, but the other girls would rather be there.

"I don't think she really is, quite," Mary Power answered. "Do you, Laura?"

"No-o," Laura said. "Not exactly. I think she just hasn't got very good judgment. But she does know everything in the books. She is a good scholar."

"Yes, she is," Mary Power agreed. "But can't a person know what is in books and still have more common sense? I wonder what is going to happen when the big boys come to school, if she can't control these little ones."

Minnie's eyes lighted up with excitement, and Ida laughed. Ida would be good and gay and laughing, no matter what happened, but Mary Power was sober and Laura was worried. She said, "Oh, we must not have trouble in school!" She must be able to study and get a teacher's certificate.

Now that Laura and Carrie were living in town, they went home at noon for a good, hot dinner. Surely the hot food was better for Carrie, though it seemed to make no difference. She was still pale and spindly, and always tired. Often her head ached so badly that she could not learn her spelling. Laura helped her with it. Carrie would know every word in the morning; then when she was called upon to recite, she would make a mistake.

Ida and Nellie still brought their dinners to school, and so did Miss Wilder. They ate together, cozily by the stove. When the other girls came back to school, Ida would join them, but Nellie often chatted with Miss Wilder through the whole noon hour.

Several times she said to the other girls, with a sly smile, "One of these days I'm going riding behind those Morgan horses, in that new buggy. You just wait and see!" They did not doubt it.

Coming in one day at noon, Laura took Carrie to the stove, to take off her wraps in the warmth. Miss Wilder and Nellie were there, talking earnestly together. Laura heard Miss Wilder say indignantly, "—school board!" Then they both saw her.

"I must ring the bell," Miss Wilder said hurriedly, and she did not look at Laura as she passed by her. Perhaps Miss Wilder had some complaint against the school board, Laura thought, and she had remembered when she saw Laura, that Pa was on the board.

That afternoon, again, Carrie missed three words in her spelling lesson. Laura's heart ached. Carrie looked so white and pitiful, she tried so hard, but it was plain to see that her head was aching terribly. It would be a little comfort to her, Laura thought, that Mamie Beardsley made some mistakes, too.

Then Miss Wilder closed her speller, and said sadly that she was disappointed and grieved. "Go to your seat, Mamie, and study this same lesson again," she said. "Carrie, you may go to the blackboard. I want to see you write, 'cataract,' 'separate,' and 'exasperate,' on the board, correctly, fifty times each."

She said it with a kind of triumph in her voice.

Laura tried to control her temper, but she could not. She was furious. It was meant as a punishment for poor little Carrie, to make her stand ashamed before the whole school. It was not fair! Mamie had missed words, too. Miss Wilder let Mamie off, and punished Carrie. She must see that Carrie did her best, and was not strong. She was mean, mean and cruel, and she was not fair!

Laura had to sit helpless. Carrie went miserably but bravely to the blackboard. She was trembling and she had to wink back tears but she would not cry. Laura sat watching her thin hand slowly writing, one long line of words and then another. Carrie grew pale and paler, but she kept on writing. Suddenly her face went gray, and she hung on to the eraser trough.

Quickly Laura raised her hand, then she jumped up, and when Miss Wilder looked at her she spoke without waiting for permission. "Please! Carrie is going to faint."

Miss Wilder turned swiftly and saw Carrie.

"Carrie! You may sit down!" she said. Sweat came out on Carrie's face and it was not so deathly gray.

155

Laura knew the worst was over. "Sit down on the front seat," Miss Wilder said, and Carrie was able to get to it.

Then Miss Wilder turned to Laura. "Since you do not want Carrie to write her misspelled words, Laura, you may go to the board and write them."

The whole school was frozen silent, looking at Laura. It was a disgrace for her, one of the big girls, to stand at the blackboard writing words as a punishment. Miss Wilder looked at Laura, too, and Laura looked straight back.

Then she went to the blackboard and took the chalk. She began to write. She felt her face grow flaming hot, but after a moment she knew that no one was jeering at her. She went on rapidly writing the words, all alike, one below another.

Several times she heard behind her a low, repeated, "Sssst! Sssst!" The whole room was noisy, as usual. Then she heard a whispered, "Laura! Sssst!"

Charley was signaling to her. He whispered, "Sssst! Don't do it! Tell her you won't do it! We'll all stand by you!"

Laura was warmed all through. But the one thing that must not happen was trouble in school. She smiled and frowned and shook her head at Charley. He sank back, disappointed but quiet. Then suddenly Laura's eye caught a furious glance from Miss Wilder. Miss Wilder had seen the whole thing.

Laura turned to the blackboard and went on writing. Miss Wilder said nothing to her or to Charley. Laura thought resentfully, "She has no right to be mad at me. She might have the grace to appreciate my trying to help keep order in school."

After school that evening Charley and his chums, Clarence and Alfred, walked close behind Laura and Mary Power and Minnie.

"I'll fix that old meanie tomorrow!" Clarence bragged, loudly, so that Laura would hear him. "I'm going to put a bent pin in her chair."

"I'll break her ruler beforehand," Charley promised him. "So she can't punish you if she catches you."

Laura turned around and walked backward. "Please don't do that, boys. Please," she asked them.

"Aw, why not? It'll be fun, and she won't do anything to us," Charley argued.

"But where is the fun?" Laura said. "That is no way for you boys to treat a woman, even if you don't like her. I do wish you wouldn't."

"We-e-ll," Clarence gave in. "Oh, all right. I won't, then."

"Then we won't, either," Alfred and Charley agreed. Laura knew they would keep their word, though they didn't want to.

Studying her lessons by the lamp that night, Laura looked up to say, "Miss Wilder doesn't like Carrie nor me, and I don't know why."

Ma paused in her knitting. "You must imagine it, Laura," she said.

Pa looked over the edge of his paper. "See that you don't give her any reason, and you'll soon feel differently."

"I don't give her any reason not to like me, Pa," Laura said earnestly. "Maybe Nellie Oleson influences her," she added, bending her head again over her book, and to herself she thought, "She listens too much to Nellie Oleson."

Laura and Carrie were early at school next morning. Miss Wilder and Nellie were sitting together by the stove. No one else was there. Laura said good morning, and as she went into the warmth of the stove her skirt brushed against the coal hod and caught on its broken rim.

"Oh, bother!" Laura exclaimed as she stood to loosen it.

"Did you tear your dress, Laura?" Miss Wilder asked acidly. "Why don't you get us a new coal hod, since your father is on the school board and you can have everything as you want it?"

Laura looked at her in amazement. "Why, no, I can't!" she exclaimed. "But likely you could have a new coal hod if you want one."

"Oh, thank you," said Miss Wilder.

Laura could not understand why Miss Wilder spoke to her in that way. Nellie pretended to be intent on a book, but a sly smile was at the corner of her mouth. Laura could not think what to say, so she said nothing.

All that morning the room was restless and noisy, but the boys kept their promise. They were no naughtier than usual. They did not know their lessons, for they would not study, and Miss Wilder was so harassed that Laura pitied her.

The afternoon began more quietly. Laura was intent on her geography lesson. Glancing up, while she memorized and thought about the exports of Brazil, she saw Carrie and Mamie Beardsley buried in study. Their heads were together over their spelling book, their eyes were fixed upon it, and their lips silently moved as they spelled the words to themselves. They did not know that they were swaying back and forth, and that their seat was swaying a little with them.

The bolts that should fasten the seat to the floor must be loose, Laura thought. The movement of the seat made no sound, so it did not matter. Laura looked at her book again and thought about seaports.

Suddenly she heard Miss Wilder speak sharply. "Carrie and Mamie! You may put away your books, and just rock that seat!"

Laura looked up. Carrie's eyes and mouth were open in surprise. Her peaked little face was white from shock, then red with shame. She and Mamie put away their speller and rocked the seat, meekly and still quietly.

"We must have quiet in order to study," Miss Wilder explained sweetly. "Hereafter anyone who disturbs us may continue that disturbance until he or she is thoroughly tired of making it."

Mamie did not mind so much, but Carrie was so ashamed that she wanted to cry.

"Go on rocking that seat, girls, till I give you leave to stop," said Miss Wilder, with that queer triumphant tone in her voice again. She turned to the blackboard, where she was explaining an arithmetic problem to the boys, who paid no attention.

Laura tried again to think about Brazil, but she could not. After a moment, Mamie gave a little toss of her head and boldly moved across the aisle into another seat.

Carrie went on rocking, but the double seat was too heavy for one little girl to rock from one end. Slowly its motion stopped.

"Keep on rocking, Carrie," Miss Wilder said sweetly. She said nothing to Mamie.

Laura's face flushed hot with fury. She did not even try to control her temper. She hated Miss Wilder, for her unfairness and her meanness. There sat Mamie, refusing to take her share of the punishment, and Miss Wilder did not say a word to her. Carrie was not strong enough to rock the heavy seat alone. Laura could hardly control herself. She bit her lip hard, and sat still.

Surely, she thought, Carrie will be excused soon. Carrie was white. She was doing her best to keep the seat rocking, but it was too heavy. Its movement grew less, and less. At last with all her strength Carrie could hardly move it at all.

"Faster, Carrie! Faster!" Miss Wilder said. "You wanted to rock the seat. Now do it."

Laura was on her feet. Her fury took possession of her, she did not try to resist it, she gave way completely. "Miss Wilder," she cried, "if you want that seat rocked faster, I'll rock it for you!"

Miss Wilder pounced on that gladly. "You may do just that! You needn't take your book, just rock that seat."

Laura hurried down the aisle. She whispered to Carrie, "Sit still and rest." She braced her feet solidly on the floor, and she rocked.

Not for nothing had Pa always said that she was as strong as a little French horse.

"THUMP!" went the back legs on the floor.

"THUMP!" the front legs came down.

All the bolts came quite loose, and

"THUMP, THUMP! THUMP, THUMP!" the seat went in rhythm, while gladly Laura rocked and Carrie sat resting.

Not even the swinging weight eased Laura's fury. She grew angrier and angrier, while louder and faster she rocked.

"THUMP, THUMP! THUMP, THUMP!"
No one could study now.

"THUMP, THUMP! THUMP, THUMP!"
Miss Wilder could hardly hear her own voice. Loudly
she called the Third Reader class.

"THUMP, THUMP! THUMP, THUMP!"
No one could recite, no one could even be heard.

"THUMP, THUMP! THUMP, THUMP! THUMP—"
Loudly Miss Wilder said, "Laura, you and Carrie are

excused from school. You may go home for the rest of the day."

"THUMP!" Laura made the seat say. Then there was dead silence.

Everyone had heard of being sent home from school. No one there had seen it done before. It was a punishment worse than whipping with a whip. Only one punishment was more dreadful; that was to be expelled from school.

Laura held her head up, but she could hardly see. She gathered Carrie's books together. Carrie followed shrinking behind her and waited trembling by the door while Laura took her own books. There was not a sound in the room. From sympathy, Mary Power and Minnie did not look at Laura. Nellie Oleson, too, was intent on a book, but the sly smile quivered at the corner of her mouth. Ida gave Laura one stricken glance of sympathy.

Carrie had opened the door, Laura walked out, and shut it behind them.

In the entry, they put on their wraps. Outside the schoolhouse everything seemed strange and empty because no one else was there, no one was on the road to town. The time was about two o'clock, when they were not expected at home.

"Oh, Laura, what will we do?" Carrie asked forlornly.

"We'll go home, of course," Laura replied. They

were going home; already the schoolhouse was some distance behind them.

"What will Pa and Ma say?" Carrie quavered.

"We'll know when they say it," said Laura. "They won't blame you, this isn't your fault. It's my fault because I rocked that seat so hard. I'm glad of it!" she added. "I'd do it again!"

Carrie did not care whose fault it was. There is no comfort anywhere for anyone who dreads to go home.

"Oh, Laura!" Carrie said. Her mittened hand slid into Laura's, and hand in hand they went on, not saying anything more. They crossed Main Street and walked up to the door. Laura opened it. They went in.

Pa turned from his desk where he was writing. Ma rose up from her chair and her ball of yarn rolled across the floor. Kitty pounced on it gaily.

"*What in the world?*" Ma exclaimed. "Girls, what is the matter? Is Carrie sick?"

"We were sent home from school," Laura said.

Ma sat down. She looked helplessly at Pa. After a dreadful stillness, Pa asked, "Why?" and his voice was stern.

"It was my fault, Pa," Carrie quickly answered. "I didn't mean to, but it was. Mamie and I began it."

"No, it's all my fault," Laura contradicted. She told what had happened. When she had finished, the stillness was dreadful again.

Then Pa spoke sternly. "You girls will go back to

school tomorrow morning, and go on as though none of this had happened. Miss Wilder may have been wrong, but she is the teacher. I cannot have my girls making trouble in school."

"No, Pa. We won't," they promised.

"Now take off your school dresses and settle down to your books," said Ma. "You can study here, the rest of the afternoon. Tomorrow you'll do as Pa says, and likely it will all blow over."

THE
SCHOOL BOARD'S VISIT

Laura thought that Nellie Oleson looked surprised and disappointed when she and Carrie came into the schoolhouse next morning. Nellie might have expected that they would not come back to school.

"Oh, I'm glad you've come back!" Mary Power said, and Ida gave Laura's arm a warm little squeeze.

"You wouldn't let her meanness keep you away from school, would you, Laura?" Ida said.

"I wouldn't let anything keep me from getting an education," Laura replied.

"I guess you wouldn't get an education if you were expelled from school," Nellie put in.

Laura looked at her. "I've done nothing to be expelled for, and I won't do anything."

"You couldn't be, anyway, could you, with your father on the school board," said Nellie.

"I wish you'd stop talking about Pa's being on the school board!" Laura burst out. "I don't know what business it is of yours if—" The bell began to ring then, and they all went to their seats.

Carrie was carefully good, and in obedience to Pa, Laura was well-behaved, too. She did not think then of the Bible verse that speaks of the cup and the platter that were clean only on the outside, but the truth is that she was like that cup and platter. She hated Miss Wilder. She still felt a burning resentment against Miss Wilder's cruel unfairness to Carrie. She wanted to get even with her. Outside, she was shining clean with good behavior, but she made not the least effort to be truly good inside.

The school had never been so noisy. All over the room there was a clatter of books and feet and a rustle of whispering. Only the big girls and Carrie sat still and studied. Whichever way Miss Wilder turned, unruliness and noise swelled up behind her. Suddenly there was a piercing yell.

Charley had leaped to his feet. His hands were clapped to the seat of his trousers. "A pin!" he yelled. "A pin in my seat!"

He held up a bent pin for Miss Wilder to see.

Her lips pressed tight together. This time she did not smile. Sharply she said, "You may come here, Charley."

Charley winked at the room, and went trudging up to Miss Wilder's desk.

"Hold out your hand," she said, as she reached inside her desk for her ruler. For a moment she felt about for it, then she looked into the desk. Her ruler was not there. She asked, "Has anyone seen my ruler?"

Not a hand was raised. Miss Wilder's face went red with anger. She said to Charley, "Go stand in that corner. Face to the wall!"

Charley went to the corner, rubbing his behind as if he still felt the pin-prick. Clarence and Alfred laughed aloud. Miss Wilder turned toward them quickly, and even more quickly Charley looked over his shoulder and made such a face at her that all the boys burst out laughing. Charley was so quick that she saw only the back of his head when very quickly she turned to see what caused the laughter.

Three or four times she turned quickly this way and that, and Charley turned more quickly, making faces at her. The whole school was roaring. Only Laura and Carrie were able to keep their faces perfectly straight. Even the other big girls were strangling and choking in their handkerchiefs.

Miss Wilder rapped for order. She had to rap with her knuckles, she had no ruler. And she could not keep order. She could not watch Charley every minute, and whenever her head was turned, he made a face at her and laughter broke out.

The boys were not breaking their promise to Laura, but they were contriving to be even naughtier than they had promised not to be. And Laura did not care. Truth to tell, she was pleased with them.

When Clarence slid out of his seat and came up the aisle on all fours, she smiled at him.

At recess, she stayed in the schoolhouse. She was sure the boys were planning more mischief, and she meant to be where she could not hear them.

After recess, the disorder was worse. The boys kept paper wads and spitballs flying on their side of the room. All the smaller girls were whispering and passing notes. While Miss Wilder was at the blackboard, Clarence went down the aisle on hands and knees, Alfred followed him, and Charley, lightfooted as a cat, ran down the aisle and leap-frogged over their backs.

They looked for Laura's approval, and she smiled at them.

"What are you laughing at, Laura?" Miss Wilder asked sharply, turning from the blackboard.

"Why, was I laughing?" Laura looked up from her book and sounded surprised. The room was quiet, the boys were in their seats, everyone seemed to be busily studying.

"Well, see that you don't!" Miss Wilder snapped. She looked sharply at Laura, then turned to the blackboard, and almost everyone but Laura and Carrie burst out laughing.

All the rest of the morning, Laura was quiet and kept her eyes on her lessons, only stealing a glance at Carrie now and then. Once Carrie looked back at Laura. Laura put a finger to her lips, and Carrie bent again over her book.

With so much noise and confusion behind her whichever way she turned, Miss Wilder grew confused herself. At noon she dismissed school half an hour early, and again Laura and Carrie were asked to explain their early arrival at home.

They told of the disorder in school, and Pa looked serious. But all he said was, "You girls be very sure that you behave yourselves. Now remember what I say."

They did. Next day the disorder was worse. The whole school was almost openly jeering at Miss Wilder. Laura was appalled at what she had started, by only two smiles at naughtiness. Still she would not try to stop it. She would never forgive Miss Wilder's unfairness to Carrie. She did not want to forgive her.

Now that everyone was teasing, baiting, or at least giggling at Miss Wilder, Nellie joined in. She was still teacher's pet, but she repeated to the other girls everything that Miss Wilder said, and laughed at her. One day she told them that Miss Wilder's name was Eliza Jane.

"It's a secret," Nellie said. "She's told me a long

time ago, but she doesn't want anyone else out here to know it."

"I don't see why," Ida wondered. "Eliza Jane is a nice name."

"I can tell you why," said Nellie. "When she was a little girl, in New York State, a dirty little girl came to school and Miss Wilder had to sit with her, and"— Nellie drew the others close and whispered—"she got lice in her hair."

They all backed away, and Mary Power exclaimed, "You shouldn't tell such horrid things, Nellie!"

"I wouldn't, only Ida asked me," said Nellie.

"Why, Nellie Oleson, I did no such thing!" Ida declared.

"You did so! Listen," Nellie giggled. "That isn't all. Her mother sent a note to the teacher, and the teacher sent the dirty little girl home, so everyone knew about it. And Miss Wilder's mother kept her out of school a whole morning to fine-comb her hair. Miss Wilder cried and cried, and she dreaded so to go back to school that she walked slow and was late. At recess her whole class made a ring around her and kept yelling, 'Lazy, lousy, Lizy Jane!' And from that day to this, she just can't bear her name. As long as she was in that school, that's what anyone called her that got mad at her, 'Lazy, lousy, Lizy Jane!'"

She said it so comically that they laughed, though they were a little ashamed of doing so. Afterward, they agreed that they would never tell Nellie anything,

171

because she was two-faced.

The school was so noisy that it was not really school any more. When Miss Wilder rang the bell, all the pupils joyfully trooped in to annoy her. She could not watch every one of them at once, she could hardly ever catch anyone. They banged their slates and their books, they threw paper wads and spitballs, they whistled between their teeth and scampered in the aisles. They were all together against Miss Wilder, they delighted in harassing and baffling and hounding her and jeering.

That feeling against Miss Wilder almost frightened Laura. No one could stop them now. The disorder was so great that Laura could not study. If she could not learn her lessons, she could not get a teacher's certificate soon enough to help keep Mary in college. Perhaps Mary must leave college, because Laura had twice smiled at naughtiness.

She knew now that she should not have done that. Yet she did not really repent. She did not forgive Miss Wilder. She felt hard and hot as burning coal when she thought of Miss Wilder's treatment of Carrie.

One Friday morning Ida gave up trying to study in the confusion, and began to draw on her slate. The whole First spelling class was making mistakes on purpose and laughing at them. Miss Wilder sent the class to the board to write the lesson. Then she was caught between the pupils at the board and those in the seats. Ida was busily drawing, swinging her feet and humming a little tune in her throat without knowing it, and Laura kept her fists clamped to her ears and tried to study.

When Miss Wilder dismissed school for recess, Ida showed Laura the picture she had drawn. It was a comic picture of Miss Wilder, so well done that it looked exactly like her, only more so. Under it Ida had written,

> We have lots of fun going to school,
> Laugh and grow fat is the only rule,
> Everyone laughs until their sides ache again
> At lazy, lousy, Lizy Jane.

"I can't get the verse just right, somehow," Ida said. Mary Power and Minnie were admiring the picture and laughing, and Mary Power said, "Why don't you get Laura to help you, she makes good verses."

"Oh, will you, Laura? Please," Ida asked. Laura took the slate and the pencil, and while the others waited she thought of a tune and fitted words to it. She meant only to please Ida, and perhaps, just a little, to show off what she could do. She wrote, in the place of the verse that Ida had erased,

> Going to school is lots of fun,
> From laughing we have gained a ton,
> We laugh until we have a pain,
> At lazy, lousy, Lizy Jane.

Ida was delighted, and so were the others. Mary Power said, "I told you Laura could do it." At that moment Miss Wilder rang the bell. The whole recess had gone, as quickly as that.

The boys came in, making all the noise they could, and as Charley passed by and caught sight of the slate, Ida laughed and let him take it.

"Oh, no!" Laura cried in a whisper, but she was too late. Until noon the boys were slipping that slate from one to another, and Laura feared that Miss Wilder would capture it, with Ida's drawing and her handwriting on it. Laura breathed a great sigh of relief when the slate came slipping back, and Ida quickly cleaned it with her slate-rag.

When they all went out to the crisp, sunny outdoors to go home for dinner, Laura heard the boys chanting all along the road to Main Street,

> "Going to school is lots of fun,
>   From laughing we have gained a ton,
>   We laugh until we have a pain,
>   At LAZY, LOUSY, LIZY JANE!"

Laura gasped. She felt sick for a minute. She cried out. "They mustn't! We must stop them. Oh, Mary Power, Minnie, come on, hurry." She called, "Boys! Charley! Clarence!"

"They don't hear you," Minnie said. "We couldn't stop them, anyway."

Already the boys were separating at Main Street. They were only talking, but Laura had no more than sighed in relief when one began to chant again, and others joined in. "Going to school is lots of fun—" Both up and down Main Street they yelled,

"*LAZY, LOUSY, LIZY JANE!*"

"Oh, *why* haven't they better sense!" Laura said.

"Laura," said Mary Power, "there's just one thing to do. Don't tell who wrote that. Ida won't, I know. I won't, and Minnie won't, will you, Minnie?"

"Cross my heart," Minnie promised. "But what about Nellie Oleson?"

"She doesn't know. She was talking with Miss Wilder, the whole recess," Mary Power reminded them. "And you'll never tell, will you, Laura?"

"Not unless Pa or Ma asks me, straight out," said Laura.

"Likely they won't think to, and then nobody will ever know," Mary Power tried to comfort Laura.

While they were eating dinner, Charley and Clarence passed by, chanting that frightful verse, and Pa said, "That sounds like some song I don't know. You ever hear a song before about lazy, lousy, Lizy Jane?"

"I never did," said Ma. "It doesn't sound like a nice song."

Laura did not say a word. She thought she had never been so miserable.

Around the schoolhouse the boys were chanting that verse. Nellie's brother Willie was with them. Inside the schoolhouse Ida and Nellie were standing at the window farthest from Miss Wilder. She must have known that Nellie had told.

Nellie was furious. She wanted to know who had written that verse, but Ida had not told her and none of the others would. No doubt her brother Willie knew or would find out. He would tell her and then she would tell Miss Wilder.

After school that night, and again on Saturday, the boys could be heard chanting those words. In the bright, clear weather they were all outdoors. Laura could almost have welcomed a blizzard to shut them in. She had never felt so ashamed, for she had spread Nellie's mean tattle-telling farther than Nellie ever could have. She blamed herself, yet she still blamed Miss Wilder far more. If Miss Wilder had been only decently fair to Carrie, Laura never could have got into such trouble.

That afternoon Mary Power came to visit. Often on Saturday afternoons she and Laura visited and worked together. They sat in the pleasant, sunny, front room.

Laura was crocheting a nubia of soft white wool, for Mary's Christmas present in college, and Mary Power was knitting a silk necktie for her father's Christmas. Ma rocked and knitted, or sometimes read interesting bits to them from the church paper, *The Advance.* Grace played about, and Carrie sewed a nine-patch quilt block.

Those were such pleasant afternoons. The winter sunshine streamed in. The room was pleasantly warm from the coal heater. Kitty, grown now to a cat, stretched and lazily purred in the sunshine on the rag rug, or curved purring against the front door, asking with a mrrreow to be let out to watch for dogs.

Kitty had become famous in town. She was such a pretty cat, such a clean blue and white, with slender body and long tail, that everyone wanted to pet her. But she was a one-family cat. Only the family could touch her. When anyone else stooped to stroke her, she flew snarling and clawing into his face. Usually someone screeched, "Don't touch that cat!" in time to save him.

She liked to sit on the front doorstep and look about the town. Boys, and sometimes the men, would set a new dog on her to see the fun. Kitty sat placidly while the dog growled and barked, but she was always ready. When the dog rushed, she rose in air with a heart-stopping yowl and landed squarely on the dog's back with all claws sunk into it. The dog went away from there.

They went in a streak, Kitty silently riding and the dog ki-yi-yowling. When Kitty thought she was far enough from home she dropped off, but the dog went on. Then Kitty walked home with proudly upright tail. Only a new dog could be set on Kitty.

Nothing could be a greater pleasure than those Saturday afternoons, when Mary Power's friendliness was added to the coziness of home, and Kitty might furnish exciting entertainment. Now Laura could not truly enjoy even this. She sat dreading to hear the boys chanting that verse again, and in her chest was a gloomy weight.

"I should make a clean breast of it, to Pa and Ma," she thought. She felt again a scalding fury against Miss Wilder. She had not meant to do harm when she wrote that verse; she had written it at recess, not in school hours. It was all too difficult to explain. Perhaps, as Ma had said, it would blow over. Least said, soonest mended. Yet at that moment perhaps someone was telling Pa.

Mary Power was troubled, too. They both made mistakes and had to unravel stitches. Never had they accomplished so little in a Saturday afternoon. Neither of them said a word about school. All the pleasure was gone from school. They were not looking forward to Monday morning.

That Monday morning was the worst yet. There was no pretense of study. The boys whistled and cat-called, and scuffled in the aisles. All the little girls but Carrie were whispering and giggling and even moving from seat to seat. Miss Wilder's, "Quiet, please!

Please be quiet!" could hardly be heard.

There was a knock at the door. Laura and Ida heard it; they sat nearest the door. They looked at each other, and when the knock came again, Ida raised her hand. Miss Wilder paid no attention.

Suddenly a loud knock sounded on the entry's inner door. Everyone heard that. The door opened and the noise died away to silence. The room grew deathly still as Pa came in. Behind him came two other men whom Laura did not know.

"Good morning, Miss Wilder," said Pa. "The school board decided it was time to visit the school."

"It is about time that something was done," Miss Wilder returned. She flushed red and then went pale while she answered, "Good morning," to the other two men and welcomed them, with Pa, to the front of the room. They stood looking over it.

Every pupil was perfectly still, and Laura's heart pounded loud.

"We heard you have been having a little trouble," the tall, solemn man said gravely but kindly.

"Yes, and I am very glad of this opportunity to tell you gentlemen the facts of the case," Miss Wilder replied angrily. "It is Laura Ingalls who makes all the trouble in this school. She thinks she can run the school because her father is on the school board. Yes, Mr. Ingalls, that is the truth! She brags that she can run this school. She didn't think I would hear of it,

179

but I did!" She flashed a glance of angry triumph at Laura.

Laura sat dumbfounded. She had never thought that Miss Wilder would tell a lie.

"I am sorry to hear this, Miss Wilder," said Pa. "I am sure that Laura did not intend to make trouble."

Laura raised her hand, but Pa lightly shook his head at her.

"She encourages the boys to be unruly, too. That is the whole trouble with them," Miss Wilder declared. "Laura Ingalls eggs them on, in every kind of mischief and disobedience."

Pa looked at Charley and his eyes were twinkling. He said, "Young man, I hear you got punished for sitting on a bent pin."

"Oh, no, sir!" Charlie replied, a picture of innocence. "I was not punished for sitting on it, sir, but for getting up off it."

The jolly member of the school board suddenly choked a laugh into a cough. Even the solemn man's mustache twitched. Miss Wilder flushed dark red. Pa was perfectly sober. No one else felt like smiling.

Slowly and weightily, Pa said, "Miss Wilder, we want you to know that the school board stands with you to keep order in this school." He looked sternly over the whole room. "All you scholars must obey Miss Wilder, behave yourselves, and learn your lessons. We want a good school, and we are going to have it."

When Pa spoke like that, he meant what he said, and it would happen.

The room was still. The stillness continued after the school board had said good day to Miss Wilder and gone. There was no fidgeting, no whispering. Quietly every pupil studied, and class after class recited diligently in the quiet.

At home Laura was quiet, too, wondering what Pa would say to her. It was not her place to speak of what had happened, until he did. He said nothing about it until the supper dishes were washed and

181

they were all settled for the evening around the lamp.

Then laying down his paper he looked at Laura and said slowly, "It is time for you to explain what you said to anyone, that you could give Miss Wilder the idea that you thought you could run the school because I am on the school board."

"I didn't say such a thing, and I did not think so, Pa," Laura said earnestly.

"I know you didn't," said Pa. "But there was something that gave her such an idea. Think what it could have been."

Laura tried to think. She was not prepared for this question, for she had been defending herself in her mind and declaring that Miss Wilder had told a lie. She had not looked for the reason why Miss Wilder told it.

"Did you speak to anyone about my being on the school board?" Pa prompted her.

Nellie Oleson had often spoken of that, but Laura had only wished that she wouldn't. Then she remembered the quarrel, when Nellie had almost slapped her. She said, "Nellie Oleson told me that Miss Wilder said you haven't much to say about the school, even if you are on the school board. And I said—"

She had been so angry that it was hard to remember exactly what she had said. "I said that you have as much to say about the school as anybody. Then I said,

'It's too bad your father doesn't own a place in town. Maybe if you weren't just country folks, your father could be on the school board.'"

"Oh, Laura," Ma said sorrowfully. "That made her angry."

"I wanted to," said Laura. "I meant to make her mad. When we lived on Plum Creek she was always making fun of Mary and me because we were country girls. She can find out what it feels like, herself."

"Laura, Laura," Ma protested in distress. "How can you be so unforgiving? That was years ago."

"She was impudent to you, too. And mean to Jack," Laura said, and tears smarted in her eyes.

"Never mind," Pa said. "Jack was a good dog and he's gone to his reward. So Nellie twisted what you said and told it to Miss Wilder, and that's made all this trouble. I see." He took up his paper. "Well, Laura, maybe you have learned a lesson that is worth while. Just remember this, 'A dog that will fetch a bone, will carry a bone.'"

For a little while there was silence, and Carrie began to study her spelling. Then Ma said, "If you will bring me your album, Laura, I would like to write in it."

Laura fetched her album from her box upstairs, and Ma sat at the desk and carefully wrote in it with her little pearl-handled pen. She dried the page carefully over the lamp, and returned the album to Laura.

On the smooth, cream-colored page, in Ma's fine

handwriting, Laura read:

> If wisdom's ways you wisely seek,
> Five things observe with care,
> To whom you speak,
> Of whom you speak,
> And how, and when, and where
>
> Your loving mother
> C L Ingalls
>
> De Smet November 15th, 1881

NAME CARDS

After all the preparation for winter, it seemed that there would be no winter. The days were clear and sunny. The frozen ground was bare of snow.

The fall term of school ended and Miss Wilder went back to Minnesota. The new teacher, Mr. Clewett, was quiet but firm, a good disciplinarian. There was not a sound in school now, except the low voices of classes reciting, and in the rows of seats every pupil diligently studied.

All the big boys were coming to school. Cap Garland was there, his face tanned dark red-brown and his pale hair and pale blue eyes seeming almost white. His smile still flashed quick as lightning and warmer than sunshine. Everyone remembered that he had made the terrible trip with Almanzo Wilder, last winter, to bring the wheat that saved them all from dying of hunger. Ben Woodworth came back to school, and Fred Gilbert, whose father had brought in the last mail after the trains stopped running, and Arthur Johnson, Minnie's brother.

Still there was no snow. At recess and at noon the boys played baseball, and the big girls did not play outdoors anymore.

Nellie worked at her crocheting. Ida and Minnie and Mary Power stood at the window, watching the ball games. Sometimes Laura stood with them, but usually she stayed at her desk and studied. She had a feeling of haste, almost of fear, that she would not be able to pass the examinations and get a teacher's certificate when she was sixteen. She was almost fifteen now.

"Oh, come on, Laura. Come watch this ball game," Ida coaxed one noon. "You have a whole year to study before you need to know so much."

Laura closed her book. She was happy that the girls wanted her. Nellie scornfully tossed her head. "I'm glad I don't have to be a teacher," she said. "My folks can get along without my having to work."

With an effort Laura held her voice low and answered sweetly. "Of course you needn't, Nellie, but you see, we aren't poor relations being helped out by our folks back east."

Nellie was so angry that she stammered as she tried to speak, and Mary Power interrupted her coolly. "If Laura wants to teach school, I don't know that it's anybody's business. Laura is smart. She will be a good teacher."

"Yes," Ida said, "She's far ahead of—" She stopped because the door opened and Cap Garland came in. He had come straight from town and he had in his hand a small striped paper bag.

"Hello, girls," he said, looking at Mary Power, and his smile lighted up as he held out the bag to her. "Have some candy?"

Nellie was quick. "Oh, Cappie!" she cried, taking the bag. "How did you know that I like candy so much? The nicest candy in town, too!" She smiled up into his face with a look that Laura had never seen before. Cap seemed startled, then he looked sheepish.

"Would you girls like some?" Nellie went on generously, and quickly she offered each one the opened bag, then taking a piece herself, she put the bag in her skirt pocket.

Cap looked pleadingly at Mary Power, but she tossed her head and looked away. Uncertainly he said, "Well, I'm glad you like it," and went out to the ball game.

The next day at noon he brought candy again. Again he tried to give it to Mary Power, and again Nellie was too quick.

187

"Oh, Cappie, you are such a dear boy to bring me more candy," she said, smiling up at him. This time she turned a little away from the others. She had no eyes for anyone but Cap. "I mustn't be a pig and eat it all myself, do have a piece, Cappie," she coaxed. He took a piece and she rapidly ate all the rest while she murmured to Cap how nice he was, and so tall and strong.

Cap looked helpless, yet pleased. He would never be able to cope with Nellie, Laura knew. Mary Power was too proud to enter into competition with her. Angrily Laura wondered, "Must a girl like Nellie be able to grab what she wants?" It was not only the candy.

Until Mr. Clewett rang the bell, Nellie kept Cap by her side and listening to her. The others pretended not to notice them. Laura asked Mary Power to write in her autograph album. All the girls but Nellie were writing in each other's albums. Nellie did not have one.

Mary Power sat at her desk and carefully wrote, with ink, while the others waited to read the verse when she finished it. Her writing was beautiful, and so was the verse she had chosen.

> The rose of the valley may wither,
> The pleasures of youth pass away,
> But friendship will blossom forever
> While all other flowers decay.

Laura's album had many treasures in it now. There was the verse that Ma had written, and on the next page was Ida's.

> In memory's golden casket,
> Drop one pearl for me.
> Your loving friend,
>   Ida B. Wright.

Every now and then Cap looked helplessly at them over Nellie's shoulder, but they paid no attention to him or Nellie. Minnie Johnson asked Laura to write in her album, and Laura said, "I will, if you'll write in mine."

"I'll do my best, but I can't write as beautifully as Mary does. Her writing is just like copper plate," Minnie said, and she sat down and wrote.

> When the name that I write here
> Is dim on the page
> And the leaves of your album
> Are yellow with age,
> Still think of me kindly
> And do not forget
> That wherever I am
> I remember you yet.
>   Minnie Johnson.

Then the bell rang, and they all went to their seats.

That afternoon at recess, Nellie sneered at autograph albums. "They're out of date," she said. "I used to have one, but I wouldn't have one of the old things now." No one believed her. She said, "In the east, where I come from, it's name cards that are all the rage now."

"What are name cards?" Ida asked.

Nellie pretended to be surprised, then she smiled, "Well, of course you wouldn't know. I'll bring mine to school and show you, but I won't give you one, because you haven't one to give me. It's only proper to exchange name cards. Everybody's exchanging name cards now, in the east."

They did not believe her. Autograph albums could not be out of style, because theirs were almost new. Ma had brought Laura's from Vinton, Iowa, only last September. On the way home after school, Minnie Johnson said, "She's just bragging. I don't believe she had name cards, I don't believe there's any such a thing."

But next morning she and Mary Power were so eager to see Laura that they waited for her to come out of the house. Mary Power had found out about name cards. Jake Hopp, who ran the newspaper, had them at the newspaper office next to the bank. They were colored cards, with colored pictures of flowers and birds, and Mr. Hopp would print your name on them.

"I don't believe Nellie Oleson has any," Minnie still declared. "She only found out about them before we did, and she plans to get some and pretend they came from the east."

"How much do they cost?" Laura asked.

"That depends on the pictures, and the kind of printing," Mary told them. "I'm getting a dozen, with plain printing, for twenty-five cents."

Laura said no more. Mary Power's father was the tailor and he could work all winter, but now there was no carpentering work in town and would be none till spring. Pa had five to feed at home, and Mary to keep in college. It was folly even to think of spending twenty-five cents for mere pleasure.

Nellie had not brought her name cards that morning. Minnie asked her, as soon as they gathered around the stove where she was warming her hands after her long, chilly walk to school.

"My goodness, I forgot all about them!" she said. "I guess I'll have to tie a string on my finger to remind me." Minnie's look said to Mary Power and Laura, "I told you so."

At noon that day Cap did bring candy again, and as usual Nellie was nearest the door. She began to coo, "Oo-oo, Cappie!" and just as she was grasping the bag of candy, Laura reached and whisked it from her surprised hand, and gave it to Mary Power.

Everyone was startled, even Laura. Then Cap's smile lighted his whole face, he glanced gratefully at Laura and looked at Mary.

"Thank you," Mary said to him. "We will all enjoy the candy so much." She offered it to the others, while as he went out to the ball game Cap gave one backward look, a grin of delight.

"Have a piece, Nellie," Mary Power invited.

"I will!" Nellie took the largest piece. "I do like Cap's candy, but as for him—pooh! you may have the greeny."

Mary Power flushed, but she did not answer. Laura felt her own face flame. "I guess you'd take him well enough if you could get him," she said. "You knew all the time he was bringing the candy to Mary."

"My goodness, I could twist him around my finger if I wanted to," Nellie bragged. "He isn't such a much. It's that chum of his I want to know, that young Mr. Wilder with the funny name. You'll see," she smiled to herself, "I'm going riding behind those horses of his."

Yes, she surely would, Laura thought. Nellie had been so friendly with Miss Wilder, it was a wonder that Miss Wilder's brother had not invited her for a drive before now. As for herself, Laura knew she had spoiled any chance of such a pleasure.

Mary Power's name cards were finished the next week, and she brought them to school. They were beautiful. The cards were palest green, and on each was a picture of a bobolink swaying and singing on a spray of goldenrod. Beneath it was printed in black letters, MARY POWER. She gave one to Minnie, one to Ida and one to Laura, though they had none to give her.

That same day, Nellie brought hers to school. They were pale yellow, with a bouquet of pansies and a scroll that said, "For Thoughts." Her name was printed in letters like handwriting. She traded one of her cards for one of Mary's.

Next day, Minnie said she was going to buy some. Her father had given her the money, and she would order them after school if the other girls would come with her. Ida could not go. She said cheerfully, "I ought not to waste time. Because I'm an adopted child, you see, I have to hurry home to help with the housework as much as I can. I couldn't ask for name cards. Father Brown is a preacher and such things are a vanity. So I'll just enjoy looking at yours when you get them, Minnie."

"Isn't she a dear?" Mary Power said after Ida had left them. No one could help loving Ida. Laura wished to be like her, but she wasn't. Secretly she so wanted name cards that she almost felt envious of Mary Power and Minnie.

In the newspaper office Mr. Hopp in his ink-spotted apron spread the sample cards on the counter for them to see. Each card was more beautiful than the last. And Laura was mean enough to be pleased that Nellie's was among them; it proved that she had bought her cards there.

They were every pale, lovely color, some even had gilt edges. There was a choice of six different bouquets, and one had a bird's nest nestled among the flowers, two birds on its rim, and above them the word Love.

"That's a young man's card," Mr. Hopp told them. "Only a young fellow's brash enough to hand out a card with 'Love' on it."

"Of course," Minnie murmured, flushing.

It was so hard to choose among them that finally Mr. Hopp said, "Well, take your time. I'll go on getting out the paper."

He went back to inking the type and laying sheets of paper on it. He had lighted the lamp before Minnie finally decided to take the pale blue card. Then guiltily, because they were so late, they all hurried home.

Pa was washing his hands and Ma was putting supper on the table when Laura came in, breathless. Quietly Ma asked, "Where have you been, Laura?"

"I'm sorry, Ma. I only meant to take a minute," Laura apologized. She told them about name cards. Of course she did not say that she wanted some. Pa remarked that Jake was up-and-coming, bringing out such novelties.

"How much do they cost?" he asked, and Laura answered that the cheapest cost twenty-five cents a dozen.

It was almost bedtime, and Laura was staring at the wall, thinking about the War of 1812, when Pa folded his paper, laid it down, and said, "Laura."

"Yes, Pa?"

"You want some of these new-fangled name cards, don't you?" Pa asked.

"I was just thinking the same thing, Charles," said Ma.

"Well, yes, I do want them," Laura admitted. "But I don't *need* them."

Pa's eyes smiled twinkling at her as he took from his pocket some coins and counted out two dimes and a nickel. "I guess you can have them, Half-Pint," he said. "Here you are."

Laura hesitated. "Do you really think I ought to? Can we afford it?" she asked.

"Laura!" Ma said. She meant, "Are you questioning what your Pa does?" Quickly Laura said, "Oh, Pa, *thank you!*"

Then Ma said, "You are a good girl, Laura, and we want you to have the pleasures of other girls of your age. Before school tomorrow morning, if you hurry, you can run up the street and order your name cards."

In her lonely bed that night without Mary, Laura felt ashamed. She was not truly good, like Ma and Mary and Ida Brown. At that very minute she was so happy to think of having name cards, not only because they were beautiful, but partly to be meanly even with Nellie Oleson, and partly to have things as nice as Mary Power and Minnie had.

Mr. Hopp promised that the cards would be ready on Wednesday at noon, and that day Laura could hardly eat her dinner. Ma excused her from doing the dishes, and she hurried to the newspaper office. There they were, delicate pink cards, with a spray of pinker roses and blue cornflowers. Her name was printed in thin, clear type: Laura Elizabeth Ingalls.

She had hardly time to admire them, for she must not be late to school. A long block from Second Street, she was hurrying along the board sidewalk, when suddenly a shining buggy pulled up beside it.

Laura looked up, surprised to see the brown Morgans. Young Mr. Wilder stood by the buggy, his cap in one hand. He held out his other hand to her and said, "Like a ride to the schoolhouse? You'll get there quicker."

He took her hand, helped her into the buggy, and stepped in beside her. Laura was almost speechless with surprise and shyness and the delight of actually riding behind those beautiful horses. They trotted gaily but very slowly and their small ears twitched, listening for the word to go faster.

"I—I'm Laura Ingalls," Laura said. It was a silly thing to say. Of course he must know who she was.

"I know your father, and I've seen you around town for quite a while," he replied. "My sister often spoke of you."

"Such beautiful horses! What are their names?" she asked. She knew quite well, but she had to say something.

"The near one is Lady, and the other is Prince," he told her.

Laura wished he would let them go faster—as fast as they could go. But it would not be polite to ask.

She thought of speaking about the weather, but that seemed silly.

She could not think of anything to say, and in all this time they had gone only one block.

"I have been getting my name cards," she heard herself saying.

"That so?" he said. "Mine are just plain cards. I brought them out from Minnesota."

He took one from his pocket and handed it to her. He was driving with one capable hand, keeping the lines in play between his gloved fingers. The card was plain and white. Printed on it in Old English letters was, Almanzo James Wilder.

"It's kind of an outlandish name," he said.

Laura tried to think of something nice to say about it. She said, "It is quite unusual."

"It was wished on me," he said grimly. "My folks have got a notion there always has to be an Almanzo in the family, because 'way back in the time of the Crusades there was a Wilder went to them, and an Arab or somebody saved his life. El Manzoor, the name was. They changed it after a while in England, but I guess there's no way to improve it much."

"I think it is a very interesting name," said Laura honestly.

She did think so, but she did not know what to do with the card. It seemed rude to give it back to him, but perhaps he did not mean her to keep it. She held it so that he could take it back if he wanted to. The team turned the corner at Second Street. In a panic Laura wondered whether, if he did not take back his card, she should give him one of hers. Nellie had said it was proper to exchange name cards.

She held his card a little nearer to him, so that he could see it plainly. He went on driving.

"Do you—do you want your card back?" Laura asked him.

"You can keep it if you want to," he replied.

"Then do you want one of mine?" She took one out of the package and gave it to him.

He looked at it and thanked her. "It is a very pretty card," he said as he put it in his pocket.

They were at the schoolhouse. He held the reins while he sprang out of the buggy, took off his cap and offered his hand to help her down. She did not need help; she barely touched his glove with her mitten-tip as she came lightly to the ground.

"Thank you for the ride," she said.

"Don't mention it," he answered. His hair was not

black, as she had thought. It was dark brown, and his eyes were such a dark blue that they did not look pale in his darkly tanned face. He had a steady, dependable, yet light-hearted look.

"Hullo, Wilder!" Cap Garland greeted him and he waved in answer as he drove away. Mr. Clewett was ringing the bell, and the boys were trooping in.

As Laura slipped into her seat, there was barely time for Ida to squeeze her arm delightedly and whisper, "Oh, I *wish* you could have seen her face! when you came driving up!"

Mary Power and Minnie were beaming at Laura across the aisle, but Nellie was looking intently away from her.

THE SOCIABLE

One Saturday afternoon Mary Power came blowing in to see Laura. Her cheeks were pink with excitement. The Ladies' Aid Society was giving a dime sociable in Mrs. Tinkham's rooms over the furniture store, next Friday night.

"I'll go if you do, Laura," Mary Power said. "Oh, please may she, Mrs. Ingalls?"

Laura did not like to ask what a dime sociable was. Fond as she was of Mary Power, she felt at a slight disadvantage with her. Mary Power's clothes were so beautifully fitted because her father tailored them, and she did her hair in the stylish new way, with bangs.

Ma said that Laura might go to the sociable. She

201

had not heard, until now, that a Ladies' Aid was organized.

To tell the truth, Pa and Ma were sadly disappointed that dear Rev. Alden from Plum Creek was not the preacher. He had wanted to be, and the church had sent him. But when he arrived, he found that Rev. Brown had established himself there. So dear Rev. Alden had gone on as a missionary to the unsettled West.

Pa and Ma could not lose interest in the church, of course, and Ma would work in the Ladies' Aid. Still, they could not feel as they would have felt had Rev. Alden been the preacher.

All next week Laura and Mary Power looked forward to the sociable. It cost a dime, so Minnie and Ida doubted that they could go, and Nellie said that, really, it didn't interest her.

Friday seemed long to Laura and Mary Power, they were so impatient for night to come. That night Laura did not take off her school dress, but put on a long apron and pinned its bib under her chin. Supper was early, and as soon as she had washed the dishes Laura began to get ready for the sociable.

Ma helped her carefully brush her dress. It was brown woolen, made in princess style. The collar was a high, tight band, close under Laura's chin, and the skirt came down to the tops of her high-buttoned shoes. It was a very pretty dress, with piping of red around wrists and collar, and the buttons all down the front were of brown horn, with a tiny raised castle in the center of each one.

Standing before the looking glass in the front room, where the lamp was, Laura carefully brushed and braided her hair, and put it up and took it down again. She could not arrange it to suit her.

"Oh, Ma, I do wish you would let me cut bangs," she almost begged. "Mary Power wears them, and they are so stylish."

"Your hair looks nice the way it is," said Ma. "Mary Power is a nice girl, but I think the new hair style is well called a 'lunatic fringe.'"

"Your hair looks beautiful, Laura," Carrie consoled her. "It's such a pretty brown and so long and thick, and it shines in the light."

Laura still looked unhappily at her reflection. She thought of the short hairs always growing at the edge around her forehead. They did not show when they were brushed back, but now she combed them all out and downward. They made a thin little fringe.

"Oh, please, Ma," she coaxed. "I wouldn't cut a heavy bang like Mary Power's, but please let me cut just a little more, so I could curl it across my forehead."

"Very well, then," Ma gave her consent.

Laura took the shears from Ma's workbasket and

standing before the glass she cut the hair above her forehead into a narrow fringe about two inches long. She laid her long slate pencil on the heater, and when it was heated she held it by the cool end and wound

wisps of the short hair around the heated end. Holding each wisp tightly around the pencil, she curled all the bangs.

The rest of her hair she combed smoothly back and braided. She wound the long braid flatly around and around on the back of her head and snugly pinned it.

"Turn around and let me see you," Ma said.

Laura turned. "Do you like it, Ma?"

"It looks quite nice," Ma admitted. "Still, I liked it better before it was cut."

"Turn this way and let me see," said Pa. He looked at her a long minute and his eyes were pleased. "Well, if you must wear this 'lunatic fringe,' I think you've made a good job of it." And Pa turned again to his paper.

"I think it is pretty. You look very nice," Carrie said softly.

Laura put on her brown coat and set carefully over her head her peaked hood of brown woolen lined with blue. The brown and the blue edges of cloth were pinked, and the hood had long ends that wound around her neck like a muffler.

She took one more look in the glass. Her cheeks were pink with excitement, and the curled bangs were stylish under the hood's blue lining that made her eyes very blue.

Ma gave her a dime and said, "Have a pleasant time, Laura. I am sure you will remember your manners."

Pa asked, "Had I better go with her as far as the door, Caroline?"

"It's early yet, and only across the street, and she's going with Mary Power," Ma answered.

Laura went out into the dark and starry night. Her heart was beating fast with anticipation. Her breath puffed white in the frosty air. Lamplight made glowing patches on the sidewalk in front of the hardware store and the drugstore, and above the dark furniture store two windows shone bright. Mary Power came out of the tailor shop, and together they climbed the outdoor stairs between it and the furniture store.

Mary Power knocked on the door, and Mrs. Tinkham opened it. She was a tiny woman, in a black dress with white lace ruffles at throat and wrists. She said good evening, and took Mary Power's dime and Laura's. Then she said, "Come this way to leave your wraps."

All the week Laura had hardly been able to wait to see what a sociable was, and now she was here. Some people were sitting in a lighted room. She felt embarrassed as she hurriedly followed Mrs. Tinkham past them into a small bedroom. She and Mary Power laid their coats and hoods on the bed. Then quietly they slipped into chairs in the larger room.

Mr. and Mrs. Johnson sat on either side of the window. The window had dotted-Swiss curtains, and before it stood a polished center table, holding a large glass lamp with a white china shade on which red roses were printed. Beside the lamp lay a green plush photograph album.

A bright flowered carpet covered the whole floor. A tall shining heater with isinglass windows stood in its center. The chairs around the walls were all of polished woods. Mr. and Mrs. Woodworth were sitting on a sofa with shining high wooden back and ends and a glittering black haircloth seat.

Only the walls of boards were like those in the front room at home, and these were thickly hung with pictures of people and places that Laura did not know. Some had wide, heavy, gilded frames. Of course Mr. Tinkham owned the furniture store.

Cap Garland's older sister Florence was there, with their mother. Mrs. Beardsley was there, and Mrs. Bradley, the druggist's wife. They all sat dressed up and silent. Mary Power and Laura did not speak, either. They did not know what to say.

Someone knocked at the door. Mrs. Tinkham hurried to it, and Rev. and Mrs. Brown came in. His rumbling voice filled the room with greetings to everyone, and then he talked with Mrs. Tinkham about the home he had left in Massachusetts.

"Not much like this place," he said. "But we are all strange here."

He fascinated Laura. She did not like him. Pa said he claimed to be a cousin of John Brown of Ossawatomie who had killed so many men in Kansas and finally succeeded in starting the Civil War. Rev. Brown did look just like the picture of John Brown in Laura's history book.

His face was large and bony. His eyes were sunk deep under shaggy white eyebrows and they shone hot and fierce even when he was smiling. His coat hung loose on his big body, his hands at the end of the sleeves were large and rough with big knuckles. He was untidy. Around his mouth his long white beard was stained yellow as if with dribbling tobacco juice.

He talked a great deal, and after he came the others talked some, except Mary Power and Laura. They tried to sit politely, but now and then they did fidget. It was a long time before Mrs. Tinkham began to bring plates from the kitchen. On each plate was a small sauce dish of custard and a piece of cake.

When Laura had eaten hers, she murmured to Mary Power, "Let's go home," and Mary answered, "Come on, I'm going." They set their empty dishes on a small table near them, put on their coats and hoods, and said good-by to Mrs. Tinkham.

Down on the street once more, Laura drew a deep breath. "Whew! If that is a sociable, I don't like sociables."

"Neither do I," Mary Power agreed. "I wish I hadn't gone. I'd rather have the dime."

Pa and Ma looked up in surprise when Laura came in, and Carrie eagerly asked, "Did you have a good time, Laura?"

"Well, no, I didn't," Laura had to admit. "You should have gone, Ma, instead of me. Mary Power and I were the only girls there. We had no one to talk to."

"This is only the first sociable," Ma made excuse. "No doubt when folks here are better acquainted, the sociables will be more interesting. I know from reading *The Advance* that church sociables are greatly enjoyed."

LITERARIES

Christmas was near, yet there was still no snow. There had not been a single blizzard. In the mornings the frozen ground was furry white with hoarfrost, but it vanished when the sun rose. Only the underneath of the sidewalk and the shadows of the stores were frosty when Laura and Carrie hurried to school. The wind nipped their noses and chilled their mittened hands and they did not try to talk through their mufflers.

The wind had a desolate sound. The sun was small and the sky was empty of birds. On the endless dull prairie the grasses lay worn-out and dead. The schoolhouse looked old and gray and tired.

It seemed that the winter would never begin and

never end. Nothing would ever happen but going to school and going home, lessons at school and lessons at home. Tomorrow would be the same as today, and in all her life, Laura felt, there would never be anything but studying and teaching school. Even Christmas would not be a real Christmas without Mary.

The book of poems, Laura supposed, was still hidden in Ma's bureau drawer. Every time Laura passed the bureau at the head of the stairs in Ma's room, she thought of that book and the poem she had not finished reading. "Courage!" he said, and pointed to the land, "This mounting wave will roll us shoreward soon." She had thought the same thought so often that it was stale, and even looking forward to the book for Christmas was no longer exciting.

Friday night came again. Laura and Carrie washed the dishes as usual. As usual, they brought their books to the lamplit table. Pa was in his chair, reading the paper. Ma was gently rocking and her knitting needles were clicking as they always did. As usual, Laura opened her history book.

Suddenly she could not bear it all. She thrust back her chair, slammed her book shut and thumped it down on the table. Pa and Ma started, and looked at her in surprise.

"I don't care!" she cried out. "I don't want to study! I don't want to learn! I don't want to teach school, *ever!*"

Ma looked as stern as it was possible for her to look. "Laura," she said, "I know you would not swear, but losing your temper and slamming things is as bad as saying the words. Let us have no more wooden swearing."

Laura did not answer.

"What is the matter, Laura?" Pa asked. "Why don't you want to learn, and to teach school?"

"Oh, I don't know!" Laura said in despair. "I am so tired of everything. I want—I want something to happen. I want to go West. I guess I want to just play, and I know I am too old," she almost sobbed, a thing she never did.

"Why, Laura!" Ma exclaimed.

"Never mind," Pa said soothingly. "You have been studying too hard, that is all."

"Yes, put away your books for this evening," said Ma. "In the last bundle of *Youth's Companions*, there are still some stories that we have not read. You may read one to us, Laura, wouldn't you like that?"

"Yes, Ma," Laura answered hopelessly. Even reading a story was not what she wanted. She did not know what she wanted, but she knew she could not have it, whatever it was. She got the *Youth's Companions* and pulled her chair to the table again. "You choose the story you want, Carrie," she said.

Patiently she read aloud, while Carrie and Grace listened wide-eyed and Ma's rocker swayed and her knitting needles clicked. Pa had gone across the street, to spend an evening talking with the men around the stove in Fuller's hardware store.

Suddenly the door opened and Pa burst in, saying, "Put on your bonnets, Caroline and girls! There's a meeting at the schoolhouse!"

"Whatever in the world—" Ma said.

"Everybody's going!" said Pa. "We are starting a literary society."

Ma laid aside her knitting. "Laura and Carrie, get your wraps on while I bundle up Grace."

Quickly they were ready to follow Pa's lighted lantern. When Ma blew out the lamp, Pa picked it up. "Better take it along, we'll want lights in the schoolhouse," he explained.

Other lanterns were coming along Main Street, and bobbing into the darkness of Second Street ahead. Pa called for Mr. Clewett, who was there and had brought the schoolhouse key. The desks looked weird in flickering lantern light. Others had brought lamps, too. Mr. Clewett lighted a large one on his desk, and Gerald Fuller drove a nail into the wall and hung up a lamp with a tin reflector. He had closed his store for the meeting. All the storekeepers were closing their stores and coming. Almost everyone in town was coming. Pa's lamp helped the lanterns to make the schoolhouse quite light.

The seats were filled and men were standing thick

213

behind them, when Mr. Clewett called the room to order. He said that the purpose of this meeting was to organize a literary society.

"The first thing in order," he said, "will be a roll call of members. I will then hear nominations for temporary chairman. The temporary chairman will take charge, and we will then proceed to nominate and ballot for permanent officers."

Everyone was a little taken aback, and felt less jolly, but it was an interesting question, who could be elected President. Then Pa stood up by his seat, and said, "Mr. Clewett and townfolks, what we've come here for is some fun to liven us up. It does not seem necessary to organize anything.

"From what I've seen," Pa went on, "the trouble with organizing a thing is that pretty soon folks get to paying more attention to the organization than to what they're organized for. I take it we're pretty well agreed right now on what we want. If we start organizing and electing, the chances are we won't be as well agreed on who's to be elected to fill office. So I suggest, let's just go straight ahead and do what we want to do, without any officers. We've got the schoolteacher, Mr. Clewett, to act as leader. Let him give out a program, every meeting, for the next meeting. Anybody that gets a good idea can speak up for it, and anybody that's called on will pitch in and do his share in the programs the best he can, to give everybody a good time."

"That's the ticket, Ingalls!" Mr. Clancy sang out, and as Pa sat down, a good many began to clap. Mr. Clewett said, "All in favor, say 'Aye!'" A loud chorus of "Ayes" voted that it should be so.

Then for a minute, no one knew what to do next. Mr. Clewett said, "We haven't any program for this

meeting." Some man answered, "Shucks, we aren't going home yet!" The barber suggested singing, and someone said, "You got some pupils that can speak pieces? How about it, Clewett?" Then a voice said, "How about a spelling match?" Several chimed in to that, "That's the notion!" "That's the idea! Let's have a spelling match!"

Mr. Clewett appointed Pa and Gerald Fuller as leaders. There was a good deal of joking as they took their places in the front corners of the room and began to call out names.

Laura sat anxiously waiting. The grown-ups were chosen first, of course. One by one they went up, and as the two lines grew longer, Laura grew more afraid that Gerald Fuller might call her before Pa did. She did not want to spell against Pa. At last there was the most anxious pause. It was Pa's turn to choose, and though he made a joke that set everyone laughing, Laura could see that he was hesitating. He decided, and called, "Laura Ingalls."

She hurried to take the next place in his line. Ma was already in it, above her. Gerald Fuller called then, "Foster!" Last of the grown-ups, Mr. Foster took the place opposite Laura. Perhaps Pa should have chosen him because he was grown-up, but Pa had wanted Laura. Surely, Laura thought, Mr. Foster could not be much of a speller. He was one of the homesteaders who drove oxen, and last winter he had stupidly jumped off Almanzo Wilder's horse, Lady, and let her run away while he fired at the antelope herd, though he was not within range.

Rapidly now all the school pupils were chosen, even the smallest. The two lines went from the teacher's desk all around the walls to the door. Then Mr. Clewett opened the speller.

First he gave out the primer words. "Foe, low, woe, roe, row, hero—" and he caught Mr. Barclay! Confused, Mr. Barclay spelled, "Hero; h-e, he, r-o-e, ro, hero," and the roar of laughter surprised him. He joined in it as he went to a seat, the first one down.

The words grew longer. More and more spellers went down. First Gerald Fuller's side was shorter, then Pa's, then Gerald Fuller's again. Everyone grew warm from laughter and excitement. Laura was in her element. She loved to spell. Her toes on a crack in the floor and her hands behind her, she spelled every word that came to her. Down went four from the enemy's side, and three from Pa's, then the word came to Laura. She took a deep breath and glibly spelled, "Differentiation: d-i-f, dif; f-e-r, fer, differ; e-n-t, different; i, differenti; a-t-i-o-n, ashun; differentiation!"

Slowly almost all the seats filled with breathless, laughing folks who had been spelled down. Six remained in Gerald Fuller's line, and only five in Pa's— Pa and Ma and Florence Garland and Ben Woodworth and Laura.

"Repetitious," said Mr. Clewett. Down went one from the other side, leaving the lines even. Ma's gentle voice spelled, "Repetitious: r-e, re; p-e-t, pet, repet; i, repeti; t-i-o-u-s, shius, repetitious."

"Mimosaceous," said Mr. Clewett. Gerald Fuller spelled, "Mimosaceous; m-i-m, mim; o-s-a, mimosa; t-i—" He was watching Mr. Clewett. "No, s-i-," he began again. "That's got me beat," he said, and sat down.

"Mimosaceous," said Florence Garland. "M-i-m, mim; o-s-a, mimosa; t-e—" And she had been a schoolteacher!

The next one on Gerald Fuller's side went down, then Ben shook his head and quit without trying. Laura stood straighter, waiting to spell the word. Now at the head of the other line, Mr. Foster began. "Mimosaceous: m-i, mi; m-o, mimo; s-a, sa, mimosa; c-e-o-u-s, sius, mimosaceous."

A great burst of applause rose up, and some man shouted, "Good for you, Foster!" Mr. Foster had taken off his thick jacket and he stood in his checked shirt, smiling sheepishly. But there was a glint in his eye. No one had guessed that he was a brilliant speller.

Fast and hard the words came pelting then, the tricky words from the very back of the spelling book. On the other line, everyone went down but Mr. Foster. Ma went down. Only Pa and Laura were left, to down Mr. Foster.

Not one of them missed a word. In breathless silence, Pa spelled, Mr. Foster spelled, Laura spelled, then Mr. Foster again. He was one against two. It seemed that they could not beat him.

Then, "Xanthophyll," said Mr. Clewett. It was Laura's turn.

"Xanthophyll," she said. To her surprise, she was suddenly confused. Her eyes shut. She could almost see the word on the speller's last page, but she could not think. It seemed that she stood a long time in a dreadful silence full of watching eyes.

"Xanthophyll," she said again desperately, and she spelled quickly, "X-a-n, zan; t-h-o, tho, zantho; p-h—" Wildly she thought, "Grecophil," and in a rush she ended, "-i-l-?" Mr. Clewett shook his head.

Trembling, Laura sat down. Now there was only Pa left.

Mr. Foster cleared his throat. "Xanthophyll," he said. "X-a-n, zan; t-h-o, tho, zantho; p-h-y—" Laura could not breathe. No one breathed. "-l," said Mr. Foster.

Mr. Clewett waited. Mr. Foster waited, too. It seemed that the waiting lasted forever. At last Mr. Foster said, "Well, then, I'm beat," and he sat down. The crowd applauded him anyway, for what he had done. He had won respect that night.

"Xanthophyll," said Pa. It seemed impossible now that anyone could spell that dreadful word, but Laura thought, Pa can, he *must*, he's *GOT* to!

"X-a-n, zan," said Pa; "t-h-o, tho, zantho; p-h-y—" he seemed slower, perhaps, than he was. "Double-l," he said.

Mr. Clewett clapped the speller shut. There had never been such thundering applause as that applause for Pa. He had spelled down the whole town.

Then, still warm and all stirred up, everyone was getting into wraps.

"I don't know when I've had such a good time!" Mrs. Bradley said to Ma.

"The best of it is, to think we'll have another meeting next Friday," said Mrs. Garland.

Still talking, the crowd was streaming out and lanterns went jogging toward Main Street.

"Well, do you feel some better, Laura?" Pa asked, and she answered, "Oh, yes! Oh, didn't we have a good time!"

THE WHIRL OF GAIETY

Now there was always Friday evening to look forward to, and after the second Literary, there was such rivalry between the entertainers that there was news almost every day.

The second Literary was entirely charades, and Pa carried off the honors of the whole evening. Nobody could guess his charade.

He played it alone, in his everyday clothes. Walking up the central aisle, he carried two small potatoes before him on the blade of his ax. That was all.

Then he stood twinkling, teasing the crowd, and giving hints. "It has to do with the Bible," he said. "Why, every one of you knows it." He said, "It's something you often consult." He even said, "It's

221

helpful in understanding Saint Paul." He teased, "Don't tell me you all give up!"

Every last one of them had to give up, and Laura was almost bursting with pride and delight when at last Pa told them, "It's Commentators on the Ac's."

As this sunk in, up rose a roar of laughter and applause.

On the way home, Laura heard Mr. Bradley say, "We'll have to go some, to beat that stunt of Ingalls!" Gerald Fuller, in his English way, called, "I say, there's talent enough for a musical program, what?"

For the next Literary, there was music. Pa with his fiddle and Gerald Fuller with his accordion made such music that the schoolhouse and the crowd seemed to dissolve in an enchantment. Whenever they stopped, applause roared for more.

It seemed impossible ever to have a more marvelous evening. But now the whole town was aroused, and families were driving in from the homestead claims to attend the Literaries. The men in town were on their mettle; they planned a superb musical evening. They practiced for it, and they borrowed Mrs. Bradley's organ.

On that Friday they wrapped the organ carefully in quilts and horse blankets, they loaded it into Mr. Foster's ox wagon and took it carefully to the schoolhouse. It was a beautiful organ, all shining wood, with carpeted pedals and a top climbing up in tapering wooden pinnacles, tiny shelves, and diamond-shaped mirrors. Its music rack was a lace pattern in wood, with red cloth behind it that showed through the holes, and on either side was a round place on which to set a lamp.

The teacher's desk was moved away, and that organ set in its place. On the blackboard Mr. Clewett wrote out the program. There was organ music by itself, organ music with Pa's fiddle, and organ music with the singing of quartets and duets and solos. Mrs. Bradley sang,

> "Backward, turn backward,
> Oh Time in thy flight.
> Make me a child again,
> Just for tonight."

Laura could hardly bear the sadness of it. Her throat swelled and ached. A tear glittered on Ma's cheek before she could catch it with her handkerchief. All the women were wiping their eyes, and the men were clearing their throats and blowing their noses.

Everyone said that surely nothing could be better than that musical program. But Pa said mysteriously, "You wait and see."

As if this were not enough, the church building was roofed at last, and now every Sunday there were two church services and Sunday school.

It was a nice church, though so new that it still looked raw. As yet there was no bell in the belfry, nor any finish on the board walls. Outside, they were not

LITTLE TOWN ON THE PRAIRIE

yet weathered gray, and inside they were bare boards and studding. The pulpit and the long benches with boxed-in ends were raw lumber, too, but it was all fresh and clean-smelling.

In the small entry built out from the door there was room enough to settle clothing blown awry by the wind, before going into the church, and Mrs. Bradley had lent her organ, so there was organ music with the singing.

Laura even enjoyed Rev. Brown's preaching. What he said did not make sense to her, but he looked like the picture of John Brown in her history book, come alive. His eyes glared, his white mustache and his whiskers bobbed, and his big hands waved and clawed and clenched into fists pounding the pulpit and shaking in air. Laura amused herself, too, by changing his sentences in her mind, to improve their grammar. She need not remember the sermon, for at home Pa required her and Carrie only to repeat the text correctly. Then, when the sermon was over, there was more singing.

Best of all was Hymn Eighteen, when the organ notes rolled out and everybody vigorously sang:

> "We are going forth with our staff in hand
> Through a desert wild in a stranger land,
> But our faith is bright and our hope is strong,
> And the Good Old Way is our pilgrim song."

Then, all together letting out their voices in chorus louder than the swelling organ song,

> "'Tis the Good Old Way by our fathers trod,
> 'Tis the Way of Life and it leadeth unto God,
> 'Tis the only path to the realms of Day,
> We are going home in the GOOD OLD WAY!"

With Sunday school and morning church, Sunday dinner and dishes, and going to church again in the evening, every Sunday fairly flew past. There was school again on Monday, and the rising excitement of waiting for the Friday Literary; Saturday was not long enough for talking it all over, then Sunday came again.

As if all this were not more than enough, the Ladies' Aid planned a great celebration of Thanksgiving, to help pay for the church. It was to be a New England Supper. Laura rushed home from school to help Ma peel and slice and stew down the biggest pumpkin that Pa had raised last summer. She carefully picked over and washed a whole quart of small white navy beans, too. Ma was going to make a mammoth pumpkin pie and the largest milkpan full of baked beans, to take to the New England Supper.

There was no school on Thanksgiving Day. There was no Thanksgiving dinner, either. It was a queer, blank day, full of anxious watching of the pie and the beans and of waiting for the evening. In the afternoon they all took turns, bathing in the washtub in the kitchen, by daylight. It was so strange to bathe by daylight, and on Thursday.

Then Laura carefully brushed her school dress, and brushed and combed and braided her hair and curled her bangs afresh. Ma dressed in her second-best, and Pa trimmed his whiskers and put on his Sunday clothes.

At lamp-lighting time, when they were all hungry for supper, Ma wrapped the great pan of beans in brown wrapping paper and a shawl, to keep the beans hot, while Laura bundled Grace into her wraps and hurried into her own coat and hood. Pa carried the beans, Ma bore in both hands the great pumpkin pie, baked in her large, square bread-baking tin. Laura and Carrie carried between them a basket full of Ma's dishes, and Grace held on to Laura's other hand.

As soon as they passed the side of Fuller's store they could see, across the vacant lots behind it, the church blazing with light. Wagons and teams and saddle ponies were already gathering around it, and people were going into its dimly lighted entry.

All the bracket lamps on the inside walls of the church were lighted. Their glass bowls were full of kerosene and their light shone dazzling bright from the tin reflectors behind their clear glass chimneys. All the benches had been set back against the walls, and two long, white-covered tables stretched glittering down the middle of the room.

"Oo, look!" Carrie cried out.

Laura stood stock-still for an instant. Even Pa and Ma almost halted, though they were too grown-up to show surprise. A grown-up person must never let feelings be shown by voice or manner. So Laura only looked, and gently hushed Grace, though she was as excited and overwhelmed as Carrie was.

In the very center of one table a pig was standing, roasted brown, and holding in its mouth a beautiful red apple.

Above all the delicious scents that came from those tables rose the delicious smell of roast pork.

In all their lives, Laura and Carrie had never seen so much food. Those tables were loaded. There were heaped dishes of mashed potatoes and of mashed turnips, and of mashed yellow squash, all dribbling melted butter down their sides from little hollows in their peaks. There were large bowls of dried corn, soaked soft again and cooked with cream. There were plates piled high with golden squares of corn bread and slices of white bread and of brown, nutty-tasting graham bread. There were cucumber pickles and beet pickles and green tomato pickles, and glass bowls on tall glass stems were full of red tomato preserves and wild-chokecherry jelly. On each table was a long, wide, deep pan of chicken pie, with steam rising through the slits in its flaky crust.

Most marvelous of all was the pig. It stood so life-like, propped up by short sticks, above a great pan filled with baked apples. It smelled so good. Better than any smell of any other food was that rich, oily, brown smell of roasted pork, that Laura had not smelled for so long.

Already people were sitting at the tables, filling and refilling their plates, passing dishes to each other, eating and talking. Already the rich, pale meat, steaming hot inside its rim of crackling brown fat, was being sliced away from one side of the pig.

"How much pork have you got there?" Laura heard a man ask as he passed back his plate for more, and the man who was carving answered, while he cut a thick slice, "Can't say exactly, but it weighed a good forty pounds, dressed."

There was not a vacant place at the table. Up and down behind the chairs Mrs. Tinkham and Mrs. Bradley were hurrying, reaching behind shoulders to refill cups with tea or coffee. Other ladies were clearing away used plates and replacing them with clean ones. As soon as anyone finished eating and left his place, it was taken, though the supper cost fifty cents. The church was almost full of people, and more were coming in.

This was all new to Laura. She felt lost and did not know what to do, until she saw Ida busily washing dishes at a table in a corner. Ma had begun to help wait on table, so Laura went to help Ida.

"Didn't you bring an apron?" Ida asked. "Then pin this towel on, so I can't splash your dress." Being a minister's daughter, Ida was used to church work. Her sleeves were rolled up, her dress was covered by a big apron, and she laughed and chattered while she washed dishes at a great rate and Laura swiftly wiped them.

"Oh, this supper's a great success!" Ida rejoiced. "Did you ever think we'd get such a crowd!"

"No," Laura answered. She whispered, "Will anything be left for us to eat?"

"Oh, yes!" Ida answered confidently, and she went on, low, "Mother Brown always sees to that. She's keeping back a couple of the best pies and a layer cake."

Laura did not care so much for the fruit pies and the cake, but she did hope that some of the pork might be left when her turn came to go to the table.

Some was left when Pa got places for Carrie and Grace and himself. Laura glimpsed them, eating happily, while she went on wiping dishes. As fast as she wiped plates and cups, they were whisked away to the tables, while even faster, it seemed, more dirty ones were piled around the dishpan.

"We really need help here," Ida said cheerfully. No one had expected such a crowd. Ma was fairly flying about, and so were most of the other ladies. Faithfully Laura kept on wiping dishes. She would not leave Ida to cope with them alone, though she grew hungrier and hungrier, and had less and less hope of getting anything to eat.

It was a long time before the tables began to be deserted. At last only the members of the Ladies' Aid, and Ida and Laura, were still hungry. Then plates and cups, knives and forks and spoons, were washed and wiped again, one table was set again, and they could sit down. A pile of bones lay where the pig had been, but Laura was happy to see that plenty of meat remained on them, and some chicken pie was left in the pan. Quietly Mrs. Brown brought out the kept-back layer cake and the pies.

For a little while Laura and Ida rested and ate, while the women complimented each other's cooking and said what a success the supper had been. There was a clamor of talking all along the crowded benches by the walls, and in the corners and around the stove the men stood talking.

Then the tables were finally cleared. Laura and Ida washed and wiped dishes again, and the women sorted them out and packed them into baskets with whatever food was left. It was a compliment to Ma's cooking that not a bite of the pumpkin pie nor a spoonful of the beans remained. Ida washed the baking pan and the milkpan, Laura wiped them, and Ma crowded them into her basket.

Mrs. Bradley was playing the organ, and Pa and

some others were singing, but Grace was asleep and it was time to go home.

"I know you are tired, Caroline," said Pa as he carried Grace homeward, while Ma carried the lantern to light the way and Laura and Carrie followed, lugging the basket of dishes. "But your Aid Society sociable was a great success."

"I *am* tired," Ma replied. A little edge to her gentle voice startled Laura. "And it wasn't a sociable. It was a New England Supper."

Pa said no more. The clock was striking eleven when he unlocked the door, and the next day was another school day, and tomorrow night was the Friday Literary.

It was to be a debate, "Resolved: That Lincoln was a greater man than Washington." Laura was eager to hear it, for Lawyer Barnes was leading the affirmative and his argument would be good.

"They will be educational," she said to Ma while they were hurriedly getting ready to go. She was really carrying on an argument with herself, for she knew that she should be studying. She had missed two whole evenings of study in that one week. Still, there would be a few days at Christmas, between the school terms, when she could make up for lost time.

The Christmas box had gone to Mary. In it Ma carefully placed the nubia that Laura had crocheted of soft, fleecy wool, as white as the big snowflakes falling gently outside the window. She put in the lace collar that she had knitted of finest white sewing thread. Then she put in six handkerchiefs that Carrie had made of thin lawn. Three were edged with narrow, machine-made lace, and three were plainly hemmed. Grace could not yet make a Christmas present, but she had saved her pennies to buy half a yard of blue ribbon, and Ma had made this into a bow for Mary to pin at her throat, on the white lace collar. Then they had all written a long Christmas letter, and into the envelope Pa put a five-dollar bill.

"That will buy the little things she needs," he said. Mary's teacher had written, praising Mary highly. The letter said, too, that Mary could send home an example of her bead work if she could buy the beads, and that she needed a special slate to write on, and that perhaps later they would wish her to own another kind of special slate on which to write Braille, a kind of writing that the blind could read with their fingers.

"Mary will know that we are all thinking of her at Christmas time," said Ma, and they were all happier in knowing that the Christmas box was on its way.

Still, without Mary it was not like Christmas. Only Grace was wholly joyous when at breakfast they opened the Christmas presents. For Grace there was a real doll, with a china head and hands, and little black slippers sewed on her cloth feet. Pa had put rockers on a cigar box to make a cradle for the doll, and Laura and Carrie and Ma had made little sheets and a pillow and a wee patchwork quilt, and had dressed the doll in a nightgown and a nightcap. Grace was perfectly happy.

Together Laura and Carrie had bought a German-silver thimble for Ma, and a blue silk necktie for Pa. And at Laura's plate was the blue-and-gilt book, Tennyson's *Poems*. Pa and Ma did not guess that she was not surprised. They had brought from Iowa a book for Carrie, too, and kept it hidden. It was *Stories of the Moorland*.

That was all there was to Christmas. After the morning's work was done, Laura at last sat down to read "The Lotos-Eaters." Even that poem was a disappointment, for in the land that seemed always afternoon the sailors turned out to be no good. They seemed to think they were entitled to live in that magic land and lie around complaining. When they thought about bestirring themselves, they only whined, "Why should we ever labor up the laboring wave?" Why, indeed! Laura thought indignantly. Wasn't that a sailor's job, to ever labor up the laboring wave? But no, they wanted dreamful ease. Laura slammed the book shut.

She knew there must be beautiful poems in such a book, but she missed Mary so much that she had no heart to read them.

Then Pa came hurrying from the post office with a letter. The handwriting was strange, but the letter was signed, Mary! She wrote that she placed the paper on a grooved, metal slate, and by feeling the grooves she could form the letters with a lead pencil. This letter was her Christmas present to them all.

She wrote that she liked college and that the teachers said she was doing well in her studies. She was learning to read and to write Braille. She wished that she might be with them on Christmas, and they must think of her on Christmas day as she would be thinking of them all.

Quietly the day went by after the letter was read. Once Laura said, "If only Mary were here, how she would enjoy the Literaries!"

Then suddenly she thought how swiftly everything was changing. It would be six more years before Mary came home, and nothing could ever be again the same as it had been.

Laura did no studying at all between those school terms, and January went by so quickly that she had hardly time to catch her breath. That winter was so mild that school was not closed for even one day. Every Friday night there was a Literary, each more exciting than the last.

There was Mrs. Jarley's Wax Works. From miles around, everyone came that night. Horses and wagons and saddle ponies were tied to all the hitching posts.

The brown Morgans stood covered with neatly buckled blankets, and Almanzo Wilder stood with Cap Garland in the crowded schoolhouse.

A curtain of white sheets hid the teacher's platform. When this curtain was drawn aside, a great gasp went up, for all along the wall and across each end of the platform was a row of wax figures, life-size.

At least, they looked as if they were made of wax.

Their faces were white as wax, except for painted-on black eyebrows and red lips. Draped in folds of white cloth, each figure stood as motionless as a graven image.

After some moments of gazing on those waxen figures, Mrs. Jarley stepped from behind the drawn-back curtain. No one knew who she was. She wore a sweeping black gown and a scoop bonnet, and in her hand she held the teacher's long pointer.

In a deep voice she said, "George Washington, I command thee! Live and move!" and with the pointer she touched one of the figures.

The figure moved! In short, stiff jerks, one arm lifted and raised from the folds of white cloth a wax-like hand gripping a hatchet. The arm made chopping motions with the hatchet.

Mrs. Jarley called each figure by its name, touched it with the pointer, and each one moved jerkily. Daniel Boone raised and lowered a gun. Queen Elizabeth put on and took off a tall gilt crown. Sir Walter

Raleigh's stiff hand moved a pipe to and from his motionless lips.

One by one all those figures were set in motion. They kept on moving, in such a lifeless, waxen way that one could hardly believe they were really alive.

When finally the curtain was drawn to, there was one long, deep breath, and then wild applause. All the wax figures, naturally alive now, had to come out before the curtain while louder and louder grew the applause. Mrs. Jarley took off her bonnet and was Gerald Fuller. Queen Elizabeth's crown and wig fell off, and she was Mr. Bradley. There seemed no end to the hilarious uproar.

"This is the climax, surely," Ma said on the way home.

"You can't tell," Pa said teasingly, as if he knew more than he would say. "This whole town has its ginger up now."

Mary Power came next day to visit with Laura, and all the afternoon they talked about the waxworks. That evening when Laura settled down to study she could only yawn.

"I might as well go to bed," she said, "I'm too slee—" and she yawned enormously.

"This will make two evenings you've lost this week," said Ma. "And tomorrow night there's church. We are living in such a whirl of gaiety lately that I declare— Was that a knock at the door?"

The knock was repeated, and Ma went to the door. Charley was there, but he would not come in. Ma took an envelope that he handed her, and shut the door.

"This is for you, Laura," she said.

Carrie and Grace looked on wide-eyed, and Pa and Ma waited while Laura read the address on the envelope. "Miss Laura Ingalls, De Smet, Dakota Territory."

"Why, what in the world," she said. She slit the envelope carefully with a hairpin and drew out a folded sheet of gilt-edged notepaper. She unfolded it and read aloud.

> Ben M. Woodworth
> requests the pleasure of
> your company at his home
> Saturday Evening
> January 28th
> Supper at Eight o'clock

Just as Ma sometimes did, Laura sat limply down. Ma took the invitation from her hand and read it again.

"It's a party," Ma said. "A supper party."

"Oh, Laura! You're asked to a party!" Carrie exclaimed. Then she asked, "What is a party like?"

"I don't know," Laura said. "Oh, Ma, what will I do? I never went to a party. How must I behave at a party?"

"You have been taught how to behave wherever you are, Laura," Ma replied. "You need only behave properly, as you know how to do."

No doubt this was true, but it was no comfort to Laura.

THE BIRTHDAY PARTY

All the next week Laura thought of the party. She wanted to go and she did not want to. Once, long ago when she was a little girl, she had gone to Nellie Oleson's party, but that was a little girl's party. This would be different.

At school Ida and Mary Power were excited about it. Arthur had told Minnie that it would be a birthday party, for Ben's birthday. From politeness they could hardly say a word about it, because Nellie was with them at recess, and Nellie had not been invited. She could not have come, because she lived in the country.

On the night of the party, Laura was dressed and ready at seven o'clock. Mary Power was coming to go with her to the depot, but she would not come for half an hour yet.

240

Laura tried to read again her favorite of Tennyson's poems,

> Come into the garden, Maud,
> For the black bat, night, has flown,
> Come into the garden, Maud,
> I am here at the gate alone;
> And the woodbine spices are wafted abroad
> And the musk of the rose is blown.

She could not sit still. She took one more look into the looking glass that hung on the wall. She wished so much to be tall and slim that she almost hoped to see a slender, tall girl. But in the glass she saw a small, round girl in a Sunday-best dress of blue cashmere.

At least it was a young lady's dress, so long that it hid the high tops of her buttoned shoes. The full-gathered skirt was gathered as full in the back as it could possibly be. Over it fitted the tight basque that came down in points in front and in back, and buttoned snugly with little green buttons straight up the front. A band of blue-and-gold-and-green plaid went around the skirt just above the hem, and narrow strips of plaid edged the pointed bottom of the basque and went around the wrists of the tight, long sleeves. The upstanding collar was of the plaid, with a frill of white lace inside it, and Ma had lent Laura her pearl-shell pin to fasten the collar together under her chin.

Laura could not find one fault with the dress. But,

241

oh! how she wished she were tall and willowy, like
Nellie Oleson. Her waist was as round as a young tree,
her arms were slender but round, too, and her very
small hands were rather plump and capable-looking.
They were not thin and languid like Nellie's hands.

Even the face in the glass was all curves. The chin
was a soft curve and the red mouth had a short, curving upper lip. The nose was almost right, but the least
bit of a saucy tilt kept it from being Grecian. The
eyes, Laura thought, were too far apart, and they were
a softer blue than Pa's. They were wide-open and
anxious. They did not sparkle at all.

Straight across the forehead was the line of curled
bangs. At least, her hair was thick and very long,
though it was not golden. It was drawn back smooth
from the bangs to the heavy mat of the coiled braid
that covered the whole back of her head. Its weight
made her feel really grown-up. She turned her head
slowly to see the lamplight run glistening on its brown
smoothness. Then suddenly she realized that she was
behaving as if she were vain of her hair.

She went to the window. Mary Power was not yet in
sight. Laura so dreaded the party that she felt she
simply could not go.

"Sit down and wait quietly, Laura," Ma gently ad-
monished her. Just then Laura caught sight of Mary
Power, and feverishly she got into her coat and put on
her hood.

She and Mary Power said hardly anything as they walked together up Main Street to its end, then followed the railroad track to the depot, where the Woodworths lived. The upstairs windows were brightly lighted, and a lamp burned in the telegraph office downstairs, where Ben's older brother Jim was still working. He was the telegraph operator. The electric telegraph's chattering sounded sharp in the frosty night.

"I guess we go into the waiting room," Mary Power said. "Do we knock, or just go right in?"

"I don't know," Laura confessed. Oddly, she felt a little better because Mary Power was uncertain, too. Still her throat was thick and her wrists were fluttering. The waiting room was a public place, but its door was shut and this was a party.

Mary Power hesitated, then knocked. She did not knock loudly, but the sound made them both start.

No one came. Boldly Laura said, "Let's go right in!"

As she spoke, she took hold of the door handle, and suddenly Ben Woodworth opened the door.

Laura was so upset that she could not answer his, "Good evening." He was wearing his Sunday suit and stiff white collar. His hair was damp and carefully combed. He added, "Mother's upstairs."

They followed him across the waiting room and up the stairs to where his mother was waiting in a little hall at their head. She was small as Laura, and

243

plumper, and she was daintiness itself, in a soft, thin gray dress with snowy white ruffles at throat and wrists. But she was so friendly that Laura felt comfortable at once.

In her bedroom they took off their wraps. The room was as dainty as Mrs. Woodworth. They hesitated to lay their coats on the dainty bed, with its knitted white coverlet and ruffled pillow shams. Thin, ruffled white muslin curtains were draped back at the windows, and on a little stand-table a knitted lace doily lay under the lamp. White knitted lace to match was spread on the bureau top, and white lace was draped across the top of the mirror frame.

Mary Power and Laura looked into the mirror, and with their fingers they fluffed up their bangs, slightly flattened by their hoods. Then in the friendliest way Mrs. Woodworth said, "If you've finished your primping, come into the sitting room."

Ida and Minnie, Arthur and Cap and Ben were already there. Mrs. Woodworth said, smiling, "Now when Jim comes up from work, our party will be complete." She sat down and began to talk pleasantly.

The sitting room was pleasant with shaded lamplight and cozy with warmth from the heater. Dark red cloth curtains were draped at the windows, and the chairs were not set against the wall but gathered about the stove, where the coals glowed through the isinglass of the stove's door. Besides the plush photograph album on the center-table's marble top, there were several other books standing on its lower shelf. Laura longed to look into them, but it would not be polite to be so inattentive to Mrs. Woodworth.

After a few moments Mrs. Woodworth excused herself and went into the kitchen. Then a stillness settled on everyone. Laura felt that she should say something, but she could think of nothing to say. Her feet seemed too big and she did not know what to do with her hands.

Through a doorway she saw a long table covered with a white cloth. China and silver sparkled on it, in the light of a lamp that hung suspended on long gilt chains from the ceiling. Glittering glass pendants hung down all around the edge of the lamp's milk-white shade.

It was all so pretty, but Laura could not forget her feet. She tried to draw them farther back beneath her skirts. She looked at the other girls, and knew that she must say something, for no one else could. Yet it was more than she could do, to break that silence. Her heart sank as she thought that, after all, a party was as uncomfortable as a sociable.

Then footsteps came springing up the stairs, and Jim came breezing in. He looked around at them all, and gravely asked, "Are you playing Quaker meeting?"

They all laughed. After that they were able to talk,

though all the time they heard small clinks of china from the other room where Mrs. Woodworth was moving about the table. Jim was so much at ease that he called out, "Supper ready, mother?"

"Yes, it is," Mrs. Woodworth said from the doorway. "Won't you all come into the dining room?"

It seemed that the Woodworths used that room only for eating in.

Eight places were set at the table, and on each of the plates was a soup plate full of steaming oyster soup. Ben's place was at the head of the table, Jim's at the foot. Mrs. Woodworth told each of the others where to sit, and said that she would wait on them all.

Now Laura's feet were under the table, her hands had something to do, and it was all so bright and gay that she was no longer bashful.

In the very center of the table was a silver castor holding cut-glass bottles of vinegar, mustard and pepper sauce, and tall salt- and pepper-shakers. The plate at each place was of white china with a wreath of tiny, many-colored flowers around the edge. Beside each plate a white napkin stood up, folded in such a way that it partly opened out like a large flower.

Most marvelous of all, in front of each plate was an orange. Not only that; for these oranges, too, had been made into flowers. The orange's peel had been cut down from the top in little pointed sections, and each section was curled inward and down, like a flower's red-gold petals. Held within these petals, the flesh of the orange curved up, covered with its thin, white skin.

The oyster soup alone was treat enough to make a party, and to go with it Mrs. Woodworth passed a bowl of tiny, round oyster crackers. When the last drop of that delicious soup had been spooned up and swallowed, she took away the soup plates, and she set on the table a platter heaped with potato patties. The small, flat cakes of mashed potatoes were fried a golden brown. She brought then a platter full of hot, creamy, brown codfish balls, and then a plate of tiny, hot biscuits. She passed butter in a round glass butter dish.

Mrs. Woodworth urged generous helpings, not once, but twice. Then she brought cups of coffee, and passed the cream and sugar.

After all this, she cleared the table again, and brought in a white-frosted birthday cake. She set it before Ben and placed a stack of small plates beside it. Ben stood up to cut the cake. He put a slice on each plate, and Mrs. Woodworth set one at each place. They waited then until Ben had cut his own slice of cake.

Laura was wondering about the orange before her. If those oranges were meant to be eaten, she did not know when or how. They were so pretty, it was a pity to spoil them. Still, she had once eaten part of an orange, so she knew how good an orange tastes.

Everyone took a bite of cake, but no one touched an orange. Laura thought that perhaps the oranges were to be taken home. Perhaps she could take home an orange, to divide with Pa and Ma and Carrie and Grace.

Then everyone saw Ben take his orange. He held it carefully over his plate, stripped off the petaled peeling, and broke the orange into its sections. He took a bite from one section, then he took a bite of cake.

Laura took up her orange, and so did everyone else. Carefully they peeled them, divided them into sections, and ate them with the slices of cake.

All the peelings were neat on the plates when supper was finished. Laura remembered to wipe her lips daintily with her napkin and fold it, and so did the other girls.

"Now we'll go downstairs and play games," Ben said.

As they all got up from the table, Laura said low to Mary Power, "Oughtn't we to help with the dishes?" and Ida asked right out, "Sha'n't we help wash the dishes first, Mrs. Woodworth?" Mrs. Woodworth thanked them, but said, "Run along and enjoy yourselves, girls! Never mind the dishes!"

The big waiting room downstairs was bright with light from the bracket lamps, and warm from the red-hot heating stove. There was plenty of room to play the liveliest games. First they played drop-the-

handkerchief, then they played blind-man's-buff.
When at last they all dropped panting onto the
benches to rest, Jim said, "I know a game you've
never played!"

Eagerly they all wanted to know what it was.

"Well, I don't believe it's got a name, it's so new,"
Jim answered. "But you all come into my office and
I'll show you how it's played."

In the small office there was barely room for them

all to stand in a half circle, as Jim told them to do, with Jim at one end and Ben at the other, crowded against Jim's worktable. Jim told them all to join hands.

"Now stand still," he told them. They all stood still, wondering what next.

Suddenly a burning tingle flashed through Laura; all the clasped hands jerked, the girls screamed, the boys yelled. Laura was frightfully startled. She made no sound and did not move.

All the others began excitedly to ask, "What was that? What was it? What did you do, Jim? Jim, how did you do that?" Cap said, "I know it was your electricity, Jim, but how did you do it?"

Jim only laughed and asked, "Didn't you feel anything, Laura?"

"Oh, yes! I felt it," Laura answered.

"Then why didn't you yell?" Jim wanted to know.

"What was the use?" Laura asked him, and Jim could not tell her that.

"But what was it?" she demanded, with all the others, and Jim would answer only, "Nobody knows."

Pa, too, had said that nobody knows what electricity is. Benjamin Franklin had discovered that it is lightning, but nobody knows what lightning is. Now it worked the electric telegraph, and still nobody knew what it was.

They all felt queer, looking at the little brass machine on the table, that could send its clicking messages so far and fast. Jim made one click on it. "That's heard in St. Paul," he said.

"Right now?" Minnie asked, and Jim said, "Right now."

They were standing silent when Pa opened the door and walked in.

"Is the party over?" he asked. "I came to see my girl home." The big clock was striking ten. No one had noticed how late it was.

While the boys put on their coats and caps that had been hanging in the waiting room, the girls went upstairs to thank Mrs. Woodworth and tell her good night. In the dainty bedroom they buttoned their coats and tied on their hoods and said Oh! what a good time they had had! Now that the dreaded party was over, Laura only wished that it could last longer.

Downstairs Rev. Brown had come for Ida, and Laura and Mary Power walked home with Pa.

Ma was waiting up when Laura and Pa came in.

"I can see what a good time you've had, by the way your eyes are shining," Ma smiled at Laura. "Now slip quietly up to bed, for Carrie and Grace are asleep. Tomorrow you can tell all of us about the party."

"Oh, Ma, each one of us had a whole orange!" Laura couldn't help saying then, but she saved the rest to tell them all together.

THE MADCAP DAYS

After the party, Laura hardly cared about studying. The party had made such a jolly friendliness among the big girls and boys that now at recess and noon on stormy days they gathered around the stove, talking and joking.

The pleasant days between snowstorms were even livelier. Then they all played at snowballing each other outdoors. This was not ladylike, but it was such fun! They came in panting and laughing, stamping snow from their shoes and shaking it from coats and hoods in the entry, and they went to their seats warm and glowing and full of fresh air.

Laura was having such a good time that she almost forgot about improving her opportunity in school. She stayed at the head of all her classes, but her grades were no longer 100. She made mistakes in arithmetic, sometimes even in history. Once her arithmetic grade went down to 93. Still, she thought she could make up lost time by studying hard next summer, though she knew by heart the true words:

> Lost, between sunrise and sunset,
> One golden hour, set with sixty diamond minutes.
> No reward is offered, for it is gone forever.

The little boys brought their Christmas-present sleds to school. Sometimes the big boys borrowed them, and took the girls sled-riding. The boys pulled the sleds, for there were no hills to slide down, and this winter no blizzards made big, hard snowdrifts.

Then Cap and Ben made a hand-bobsled, big enough for all four girls to crowd into. The four boys pulled it. At recess they raced at great speed, far out onto the prairie road and back. At noon they had time to go even farther.

At last Nellie Oleson could not bear standing alone at the window and watching this. She had always disdained to play outdoors in the cold that might roughen her delicate complexion and chap her hands, but one day at noon she declared that she would go for a sled ride.

The sled was not large enough for five, but the boys

would not agree to let any one of the other girls stay behind. They coaxed all five girls into the sled. The girls' feet stuck out from the sides, their skirts had to be gathered in till their woolen stockings showed above their high shoetops. Away they went, out on the snowy road.

They were windblown, disheveled, red-faced from cold and wind and laughter and excitement as the boys swung in a circle over the prairie and ran toward town, drawing the sled behind them. They whisked past the schoolhouse and Cap shouted, "Let's go up and down Main Street!"

With laughter and shouts the other boys agreed, running even faster.

Nellie shrieked, "Stop this minute! Stop! Stop, I tell you!"

Ida called, "Oh boys, you mustn't!" but she could not stop laughing. Laura was laughing, too, for they were such a funny sight, heels kicking helplessly, skirts blowing, fascinators and mufflers and hair whipping in the wind. Nellie's screaming only added to the boys' merriment as they ran the faster. Surely, Laura thought, they wouldn't go onto Main Street. Surely they would turn back any minute.

"No! No! *Arthur*, no!" Minnie was screaming, and Mary Power was begging, "Don't! Oh, please don't!"

Laura saw the brown Morgan horses standing blanketed at the hitching posts. Almanzo Wilder, in a big fur coat, was untying them. He turned to see what caused the girls' screaming, and at the same instant Laura knew that the boys meant to take them all past him, past all the eyes on Main Street. This was not funny at all.

The other girls were making such a commotion that Laura had to speak low, to be heard.

"Cap!" she said. "Please make them stop. Mary doesn't want to go on Main Street."

Cap began to turn at once. The other boys pulled against him, but Cap said, "Aw, come on," and swung the sled.

They were on their way back to the schoolhouse and the bell was ringing. At the schoolhouse door they scrambled out of the sled good-naturedly, all but Nellie. Nellie was furious.

"You boys think you're smart!" she raged. "You— you—you *ignorant westerners!*"

The boys looked at her, sober and silent. They could not say what they wanted to, because she was a girl. Then Cap glanced anxiously at Mary Power, and she smiled at him.

"Thank you, boys, for the ride," Laura said.

"Yes, thank you all, it was such fun!" Ida chimed in.

"Thank you," Mary Power said, smiling at Cap, and his flashing smile lighted up his whole face.

"We'll go again at recess," he promised, as they all trooped into the schoolhouse.

In March the snow was melting, and final examinations were near. Still Laura did not study as she should. All the talk now was about the last Literary of that winter. What it would be was a secret that everyone was trying to guess. Even Nellie's family was coming to it, and Nellie was going to wear a new dress.

At home, instead of studying, Laura sponged and pressed her blue cashmere and freshened its lace frill. She so wanted a hat to wear instead of her hood that Ma bought for her half a yard of beautiful brown velvet.

"I know you'll take the very best care of the hat," Ma made excuse to herself, "and it will be perfectly good to wear for some winters to come."

So on Saturdays Mary Power and Laura made their hats. Mary's was of dark blue cloth, trimmed with a twist of black velvet and blue, all from her father's scrap bag. Laura's was of that lovely brown velvet, so soft to touch, and with a tawny-golden sheen to its silkiness. She wore it for the first time to the Literary.

In the schoolhouse no preparation was to be seen, except that the teacher's desk had been moved from the platform. People crowded three in a seat, and every inch of standing room was jammed. Even on the teacher's desk, boys stood tightly crowded. Mr. Bradley and Lawyer Barnes pressed back the mass of people, to keep the center aisle clear. No one knew why, and no one knew what was happening when a great shout went up from the people outside who were trying to get in.

Then up the center aisle came marching five black-faced men in raggedy-taggedy uniforms. White circles were around their eyes and their mouths were wide and red. Up onto the platform they marched, then facing forward in a row suddenly they all advanced, singing,

> "Oh, talk about your Mulligan Guards!
> These darkies can't be beat!"

Backward, forward and backward and forward they marched, back and forth, back and forth.

> "Oh TALK ABOUT your MULLigan GUARDS!
> These DARKies CAN't be BEAT!
> We MARCH in TIME and CUT a SHINE!
> Just WATCH these DARKies' feet!"

The man in the middle was clog dancing. Back against the wall stood the four raggedy black-faced men. One played a jew's-harp, one played a mouth organ, one kept the time with rattling bones, and one man clapped with hands and feet.

The cheering started; it couldn't be stopped. Feet could not be kept still. The whole crowd was carried away by the pounding music, the grinning white-eyed faces, the wild dancing.

257

There was no time to think. When the dancing stopped, the jokes began. The white-circled eyes rolled, the big red mouths blabbed questions and answers that were the funniest ever heard. Then there was music again, and even wilder dancing.

When the five darkies suddenly raced down the aisle and were gone, everyone was weak from excite-

ment and laughing. It did not seem possible that the whole evening had gone. The famous minstrel shows in New York surely could not be better than that minstrel show had been. Then a question ran through the whole jostling crowd, "Who were they?"

In their rag-tag clothing and with their blackened faces, it had been hard to know who they were. Laura was sure that the clog dancer was Gerald Fuller, for she had once seen him dance a jig on the sidewalk in front of his hardware store. And as she remembered the black hands that had held the long, flat, white bones between their fingers and kept them rattling out the tunes, she would have been certain that the darky was Pa, if the darky had had whiskers.

"Pa couldn't have cut off his whiskers, could he?" she asked Ma, and in horror Ma answered, "Mercy, no!" Then she added, "I hope not."

"Pa must have been one of the darkies," Carrie said, "because he did not come with us."

"Yes, I know he was practicing to be in the minstrel show," said Ma, walking faster.

"Well, but none of the darkies had whiskers, Ma," Carrie reminded her.

"My goodness," Ma said. "Oh my goodness." She had been so carried away that she had not thought of that. "He couldn't have," she said, and she asked Laura, "Do you suppose he would?"

"I don't know," Laura answered. She really thought

that, for such an evening, Pa would have sacrificed even his whiskers, but she did not know what he had done.

They hurried home. Pa was not there. It seemed a much longer time than it was, before he came in, cheerfully asking, "Well, how was the minstrel show?"

His long brown whiskers were as they had always been.

"*What did you do with your whiskers?*" Laura cried.

Pa pretended to be surprised and puzzled, asking, "Why, what is wrong with my whiskers?"

"Charles, you'll be the death of me," Ma said, helplessly laughing. But looking closely, Laura saw the smallest white smudge in the laughing-wrinkles at the corner of his eye, and she found a very little black grease in his whiskers.

"I know! You blacked them and smoothed them down behind that high coat-collar!" she accused him, and he could not deny it. He had been the darky who rattled the bones.

Such an evening came once in a lifetime, Ma said, and they all sat up late, talking about it. There would be no more Literaries that winter, for spring was coming soon.

"We'll move back to the claim as soon as school lets out," Pa said. "How will all of you like that?"

"I must be looking over my garden seeds," Ma said thoughtfully.

"I'll be glad to go. Grace and I'll pick violets again," said Carrie. "Won't you be glad, Grace?" But Grace was almost asleep in Ma's lap in the rocking chair. She only opened one eye and murmured, "Vi'lets."

"How about you, Laura?" Pa asked. "I've been thinking that by now you might want to stay in town."

"I might," Laura admitted. "I do like living in town better than I ever thought I would. But everyone will be moving out to hold down claims all summer, and we'll come back to town next winter, won't we?"

"Yes, I really think we will," said Pa. "We might as well, as long as I can't rent this building, and it is safer for you girls going to school. Though we might as well have stayed on the claim this winter. Well, that's the way it goes. Get ready for a hard winter, and there's not so much as one blizzard."

He said it so comically that they all burst out laughing at the joke on them.

After that, there was moving to think about, and in the warming air scented with damp earth, Laura felt less than ever like studying. She knew she could pass the examinations, even if her grades were not as high as they should be.

When her conscience pricked her, she thought rebelliously that she wouldn't see Ida and Mary Power and Minnie and the boys again, all summer long. She promised herself that she would study really hard, next summer.

In the examinations she did not make one perfect grade. Her history grade was only 99, and in arithmetic she earned only 92 plus. That was her record, and she could never change it now.

Then suddenly she knew that there must be no more self-indulgence. There were only ten months left, before she would be sixteen years old. Summer was before her, with blue skies and great blowing white clouds, the violets blooming in the buffalo wallow and the wild roses spangling the prairie grasses, but she must stay in the house and study. She must. If she did not, perhaps next spring she could not get a teacher's certificate, and Mary might have to leave college.

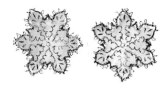

UNEXPECTED IN APRIL

Everything was settled in the little house on the homestead. Outdoors the snow was all gone, a green mist of new grass lay over the prairie, and plowed land spread black and sweet-smelling under the warm sun.

For two hours that morning Laura had studied. Now as she cleared away the dinner dishes she saw her slate and schoolbooks waiting and she felt the soft breeze beguiling her to go walking with Carrie and Grace in the spring weather. She knew she had to study.

"I think I'll go to town this afternoon," said Pa as he put on his hat. "Is there anything you want me to get, Caroline?"

Suddenly the breeze was icy cold, and Laura looked

quickly from the window. She exclaimed, "Pa! There's a blizzard cloud!"

"Why, it can't be! This late in April?" Pa turned to see for himself.

The sunlight went out, the sound of wind changed as it rose. The storm struck the little house. A whirling whiteness pressed against the window and the cold came in.

"On second thought," said Pa, "I believe I'd rather stay home this afternoon."

He drew a chair close to the stove and sat down. "I'm glad all the stock is in the stable. I was going to get picket ropes in town," he added.

Kitty was frantic. This was the first blizzard she had known. She did not know what to make of it, when all of her fur stood up and crackled. Trying to soothe her, Grace discovered that a spark would snap from her wherever she was touched. Nothing could be done about that, except not to touch her.

Three days and nights the blizzard raged. Pa put the hens in the stable lest they freeze. It was so cold that the dismal days were spent close to the stove, and though the light was dim, Laura doggedly studied arithmetic. "At least," she thought, "I don't want to go walking."

On the third day, the blizzard left the prairie covered with fine, hard snow. It was still frozen when Pa walked to town next day. He brought back news that two men had been lost in that blizzard.

They had come from the east on the train, in the warm spring morning. They had driven out to see friends on a claim south of town, and just before noon they had set out to walk to another claim two miles away.

After the blizzard, the whole neighborhood turned out to search for them, and they were found beside a haystack, frozen to death.

"Being from the east, they didn't know what to do," said Pa. If they had dug into the haystack and plugged the hole behind them with hay, they might have lived through the blizzard.

"But whoever could have expected such a blizzard, so late," said Ma.

"Nobody knows what will happen," Pa said. "Prepare for the worst and then you've some grounds to hope for the best, that's all you can do."

Laura objected. "You were all prepared for the worst last winter, Pa, and all that work was wasted. There wasn't one blizzard till we were back here and not prepared for it."

"It does seem that these blizzards are bound to catch us, coming or going," Pa almost agreed.

"I don't see how anybody can be prepared for anything," said Laura. "When you expect something, and then something else always happens."

"Laura," said Ma.

"Well, it does, Ma," Laura protested.

"No," Ma said. "Even the weather has more sense in it than you seem to give it credit for. Blizzards come only in blizzard country. You may be well prepared to teach school and still not be a schoolteacher, but if you were not prepared, it's certain that you won't be."

That was so. Later Laura remembered that Ma had once been a schoolteacher. That evening when she had put away her books to help Ma get supper, she asked, "How many terms of school did you teach, Ma?"

"Two," said Ma.

"What happened then?" Laura asked.

"I met your Pa," Ma answered.

"Oh," Laura said. Hopefully she thought that she might meet somebody. Maybe, after all, she would not have to be a schoolteacher always.

SCHOOLTIME
BEGINS AGAIN

Aterward it seemed to Laura that she did nothing but study that whole summer long. Of course this was not true. She brought water from the well in the mornings, she milked and moved the picket pins and taught the new calf to drink. She worked in the garden and in the house, and in haying time she trod down the great loads of hay that Pa drove away to town. But the long, hot, sticky hours with schoolbooks and slate seemed to overshadow all else. She didn't go to town even for Fourth of July. Carrie went with Pa and Ma but Laura stayed at home to take care of Grace and study the Constitution.

Letters came often from Mary, and every week a long letter went to her in return. Even Grace was able to write little letters, as Ma taught her, and these were always sent to Mary with the others.

The hens were laying now. Ma saved the best eggs for setting, and twenty-four chicks hatched. The smallest pullet eggs Ma used in cooking, and for one Sunday dinner, with the first green peas and new potatoes, they ate fried chickens. The other cockerels Ma let grow up. They would be larger to eat, later on.

The gophers came again, and Kitty grew fat in the cornfield. She caught more gophers than she could eat, and at all hours of the day she could be heard mrreowling proudly as she brought a fresh-killed one to lay at Ma's feet or Laura's or Carrie's or Grace's. She wanted to share her good food, and her puzzled look showed plainly that she could not understand why the whole family did not eat gophers.

The blackbirds came again. Though they were not so many this year, and Kitty caught some of them, still they did damage enough. Again the mellow fall weather came, and Laura and Carrie walked to school.

There were more people in town now, and in all the country around. The school was so crowded that all the seats were filled, and in some of the front seats three of the smaller pupils sat.

There was a new teacher, Mr. Owen, a son of the

Mr. Owen whose bay horses had almost won the Fourth of July race. Laura liked and respected him very much. He was not very old, but he was serious and industrious and enterprising.

From the first day, he ruled with a firm hand. Every pupil was obedient and respectful, every lesson was thoroughly learned. On the third day of school, Mr. Owen whipped Willie Oleson.

For some time, Laura did not quite know what she thought about that whipping. Willie was bright enough, but he had never learned his lessons. When he was called upon to recite, he let his mouth fall open and all the sense went out of his eyes. He looked less than half-witted, he hardly looked human. It made anyone turn sick to see him.

He had begun doing this, to tease Miss Wilder. He seemed unable to collect his scattered mind enough to understand anything she said to him. At recess he would do this again, to amuse the other boys. When Mr. Clewett taught, he thought that Willie was a halfwit, and required nothing of him. The habit had grown on Willie, until now at any time he could be seen mooning about with his mouth dropped open and his eyes empty. Laura really thought that Willie's mind completely left him at these times.

The first time that Willie goggled at Mr. Owen was when his name was asked for the school record. Mr. Owen was startled, and Nellie spoke up. "He's my brother, Willie Oleson, and he can't answer questions, they confuse him."

Several times that day and the next, Laura saw Mr. Owen glance sharply at Willie. Willie was always drooling and staring blankly. When he was called upon to recite, Laura could not bear to see his idiot face. On the third day, Mr. Owen quietly said, "Come with me, Willie."

He had a pointer in his hand. With the other hand firmly on Willie's shoulder, he took Willie into the entry and shut the door. He did not say anything. From their seat nearest the door, Ida and Laura heard the swish and thud of the pointer. Everyone heard Willie's howls.

Mr. Owen came quietly in with Willie. "Stop blubbering," he said. "Go to your seat and study. I expect you to know and recite your lessons."

Willie stopped blubbering and went to his seat. After that, one look from Mr. Owen cleared some of the idiot look from Willie's face. He seemed to be trying to think, and to act like other boys. Laura often wondered whether he could pull his mind together after he had let it go to pieces so, but at least Willie was trying. He was afraid not to try.

Laura and Ida, Mary Power and Minnie, and Nellie Oleson had kept their old seats. They were all tanned brown from the summer sun, except Nellie, who was paler and more ladylike than ever. Her clothes were so beautiful, though her mother did make them from castoffs, that Laura grew dissatisfied with her brown school dress and her blue cashmere for best. She did not complain, of course, but she wanted to.

Hoops had finally come in, and Ma bought a set for Laura. She let down the hem of the brown dress, and made it over so cleverly that it could be worn over hoops perfectly well, and the full blue cashmere needed no changing. Still, Laura felt that all the other girls were better dressed.

Mary Power had a new school dress. Minnie Johnson had a new coat and new shoes. Ida's clothes came out of a missionary barrel, but Ida was so sweet and merry that she looked perfectly dear in anything. When Laura dressed for school, it seemed to her that the more she fussed with her appearance the more dissatisfying it was.

"Your corset is too loose," Ma tried to help her one morning. "Pull the strings tighter and your figure will be neater. And I can't think that a lunatic fringe is the most becoming way to do your hair. It makes any girl's ears appear larger to comb the hair up back of them and to have that mat of bangs above the forehead."

Ma was anxiously helpful, but some sudden thought made her laugh softly to herself.

"What is it, Ma? Tell us!" Laura and Carrie begged.

"I was only thinking of the time your Aunt Eliza

and I combed our hair up off our ears and went to school that way. The teacher called us up front and shamed us before the whole school, for being so unladylike and bold as to let our ears be seen." Ma laughed softly again.

"Is that the reason you always wear those soft wings of hair down over your ears?" Laura cried.

Ma looked a little surprised. "Yes, I suppose it is," she answered, still smiling.

On the way to school Laura said, "Carrie, do you know I've never once seen Ma's ears?"

"They're probably pretty ears, too," said Carrie. "You look like her, and your ears are little and pretty."

"Well," Laura began; then she stopped and spun around and round, for the strong wind blowing against her always made the wires of her hoop skirt creep slowly upward under her skirts until they bunched around her knees. Then she must whirl around and around until the wires shook loose and spiraled down to the bottom of her skirts where they should be.

As she and Carrie hurried on she began again. "I think it was silly, the way they dressed when Ma was a girl, don't you? Drat this wind!" she exclaimed as the hoops began creeping upward again.

Quietly Carrie stood by while Laura whirled. "I'm glad I'm not old enough to have to wear hoops," she said. "They'd make me dizzy."

"They are rather a nuisance," Laura admitted. "But they are stylish, and when you're my age you'll want to be in style."

Living in town was so exciting that fall that Pa said there was no need of Literaries. There was church every Sunday, prayer meeting every Wednesday night. The Ladies' Aid planned two sociables, and there was talk of a Christmas tree. Laura hoped there would be one, for Grace had never seen a Christmas tree. In November, there was to be a week of revival meetings at the church, and Mr. Owen, with the school board's approval, was planning a School Exhibition.

School would go on without interruption until the School Exhibition just before Christmas. So the big boys did not wait until winter, but came to school in November. More smaller pupils had to be crowded three in a seat to make room for them.

"This school needs a larger building," Mr. Owen said to Laura and Ida one day at recess. "I am hoping that the town can afford to build one next summer. There really is a need for a graded school, even. I am counting a great deal upon the showing we make at the School Exhibition, to acquaint the people with the school and its needs."

After that, he told Laura and Ida that their part in the Exhibition would be to recite the whole of American history, from memory.

"Oh, do you think we can do it, Laura?" Ida gasped

when he had left them.

"Oh, yes!" Laura answered. "You know we like history."

"I'm glad you've got the longer part, anyway," said Ida. "I've only got to remember from John Quincy Adams to Rutherford B. Hayes, but you've got all that about the discoveries and the map and the battles, and the Western Reserve and the Constitution. My! I don't know how you ever can!"

"It's longer, but we've studied it more and reviewed it oftener," said Laura. She was glad to have that part; she thought it more interesting.

The other girls were talking eagerly about the revival meetings. Everyone in town and from all the near-by country would go to them. Laura did not know why, for she had never been to a revival meeting, but when she said she should stay home and study, Nellie exclaimed in horror, "Why, people who don't go to revival meetings are *atheists!*"

The others did not say a word in Laura's defense, and Ida's brown eyes pleaded anxiously when she said, "You are coming, aren't you, Laura?"

The revival meetings would last a whole week, and besides the daily lessons, there was the School Exhibition to prepare for. Monday night Laura hurried home from school to study till supper time; she thought about history while she washed the dishes, and then snatched a little time with her books while

Pa and Ma were dressing.

"Hurry, Laura, or we'll be late! It's church time now," said Ma.

Standing before the glass, Laura hurriedly set her darling brown velvet hat evenly on her bangs, and fluffed them out. Ma waited by the door with Carrie and Grace. Pa shut the stove's draft and turned down the lamp wick.

"Are you all ready?" he asked; then he blew out the lamp. By his lantern light they all went out, and he locked the door. Not a window on Main Street was lighted. Behind Fuller's Hardware the last lanterns were bobbing across the vacant lots toward the brightly lighted church, and wagons, buggies, and blanketed horses stood thick in the shadows around it.

The church was crowded, and hot from the dazzling lamps and the coal heater. Graybeards sat close around the pulpit, families were in the middle seats, and young men and boys filled the back seats. Laura saw everyone she knew and many strangers, as Pa led the way up the aisle, looking for a vacant place. He stopped next to the front seat, and Ma with Grace, then Carrie and Laura, edged past knees and sat down.

Reverend Brown rose from his chair behind the pulpit and gave out a hymn, Number 154. Mrs. Brown played the organ, and everyone stood up and sang.

"There were ninety and nine that safely lay
    In the shelter of the fold,
But one was out on the hills away,
    Far off from the gates of gold,
Away on the mountains wild and bare,
Away from the tender shepherd's care."

If a revival meeting could be nothing but singing, Laura would have loved it, though she felt that she should be studying, not wasting time in enjoyment. Her voice rose clear and true as Pa's, as they sang,

"Rejoice, for the Lord brings back His own!"

Then the long prayer began. Laura bent her head and closed her eyes while Reverend Brown's harsh voice singsonged on and on. It was a great relief to stand up at last, and sing again. This was a hymn with a dancing swing and a throbbing beat.

"Sowing the seed by the daylight fair,
Sowing the seed by the noonday glare,
Sowing the seed by the fading light,
Sowing the seed in the solemn night,
Oh, what shall the harvest be-e-e,
Oh, what shall the harvest be?"

Reverend Brown's preaching went on with the throbbing and swinging. His voice rose and fell, thundered and quivered. His bushy white eyebrows raised and lowered, his fist thumped the pulpit. "Repent ye, repent ye while yet there is time, time to be saved from damnation!" he roared.

Chills ran up Laura's spine and over her scalp. She seemed to feel something rising from all those people, something dark and frightening that grew and grew under that thrashing voice. The words no longer made sense, they were not sentences, they were only dreadful words. For one horrible instant Laura imagined that Reverend Brown was the Devil. His eyes had fires in them.

"Come forward, come forward and be saved! Come to salvation! Repent, ye sinners! Stand up, stand up and sing! Oh, lost lambs! Flee from the wrath! Pull, pull for the shore!" His hands lifted them all to their feet, his loud voice sang:

> "Pull for the shore, sailor!
> Pull for the shore!"

"Come! Come!" his voice roared through the storm of singing, and someone, a young man, came stumbling up the aisle.

> "Heed not the stormy winds,
> Though loudly they roar."

"Bless you, bless you, my sinning brother, down on your knees and God bless you; are there any more? Any more?" Reverend Brown was shouting, and his voice roared again into the song, "Pull for the Shore!"

The first words of that hymn had made Laura want to laugh. She remembered the tall thin man and the pudgy little one, so solemnly singing it, and all the storekeepers popping from the torn screen doors. Now she felt that all the noise and excitement was not touching her.

She looked at Pa and Ma. They were quietly standing and quietly singing, while the dark, wild thing that she had felt was roaring all around them like a blizzard.

Another young man, and then an older woman, went forward and knelt. Then church was over, yet somehow not over. People were pressing forward to crowd around those three and wrestle for their souls. In a low voice Pa said to Ma, "Come, let's go."

He carried Grace down the aisle toward the door. Ma followed with Carrie, and behind her Laura followed close. In the back seats all the young men and boys stood watching the people passing by. Laura's dread of strangers came over her and the open door ahead seemed a refuge from their eyes.

She did not notice a touch on her coat sleeve until she heard a voice saying, "May I see you home?"

It was Almanzo Wilder.

Laura was so surprised that she could not say a word. She could not even nod or shake her head. She could not think. His hand stayed on her arm and he walked beside her through the door. He protected her from being jostled in the crowded entry.

Pa had just lighted the lantern. He lowered the chimney and looked up, just as Ma turned back and asked, "Where's Laura?" They both saw Laura with Almanzo Wilder beside her, and Ma stood petrified.

"Come on, Caroline," said Pa. Ma followed him, and after one wide-eyed stare, Carrie did too.

The ground was white with snow and it was cold, but there was no wind, and stars shone brightly in the sky.

Laura could not think of a word to say. She wished that Mr. Wilder would say something. A faint scent of cigar smoke came from his thick cloth overcoat. It was pleasant, but not as homelike as the scent of Pa's pipe. It was a more dashing scent, it made her think of Cap and this young man daring that dangerous trip to bring back the wheat. All this time she was trying to think of something to say.

To her complete surprise, she heard her own voice, "Anyway, there's no blizzard."

"No. This is a nice winter, not much like the Hard Winter," said he.

Again there was silence, except for the crunch of their feet on the snow-covered path.

On Main Street, dark groups hurried homeward, with lanterns that cast big shadows. Pa's lantern went straight across the street. Pa and Ma and Carrie and

Grace went in and were at home.

Laura and Almanzo stood outside the closed door.

"Well, good night," he said, as he made a backward step and raised his cap. "I'll see you tomorrow night."

"Good night," Laura answered, as she quickly opened the door. Pa was holding the lantern up while Ma lighted the lamp, and he was saying, "—trust him anywhere, and it's only walking home from Church."

"But she's only fifteen!" said Ma.

Then the door was shut. Laura was inside the warm room. The lamp was lighted, and everything was right.

"Well, what did you think of the revival meeting?" Pa asked, and Laura answered, "It isn't much like Reverend Alden's quiet sermons. I like his better."

"So do I," said Pa. Then Ma said it was past bed-time.

Several times next day, Laura wondered what young Mr. Wilder had meant by saying that he would see her that night. She did not know why he had walked home with her. It was an odd thing for him to do, for he was a grown-up. He had been a homesteader for a few years, so he must be at least twenty-three years old, and he was Pa's friend more than hers.

That night in church she did not mind the sermon at all. She only wished she need not be there, when so many people, all together, grew so excited. She was glad when Pa said again, "Let's go."

Almanzo Wilder stood in the line of young men near
the door, and Laura was embarrassed. She saw now
that several young men were taking young ladies
home. She felt her cheeks flushing and she did not
know where to look. Again he asked, "May I see you
home?" and this time she answered politely, "Yes."

She had thought what she would have said last

night, so now she spoke about Minnesota. She had come from Plum Creek and he had come from Spring Valley, but before that he had lived in New York State, near Malone. Laura thought she kept the conversation going quite well, until they reached the door where she could say, "Good night."

Every night that week he saw her home from the revival meeting. She still could not understand why. But the week soon ended, so that again she could spend the evenings in study, and she forgot to wonder about Almanzo in her dread of the School Exhibition.

THE SCHOOL EXHIBITION

The room was warm and the lamp burned clear and bright, but Laura's chilly fingers could hardly button her blue cashmere basque and it seemed to her that the looking glass was dim. She was dressing to go to the School Exhibition.

She had dreaded it for so long that now it did not seem real, but it was. Somehow she had to get through it.

Carrie was frightened, too. Her eyes were very large in her thin face, and she whispered to herself, "'Chisel in hand stood the sculptor boy,'" while Laura tied on her hair ribbon. Ma had made a new dress of

283

bright plaid woolen for Carrie to wear when she spoke her piece.

"Ma, please hear me say my piece again," she begged.

"There isn't time, Carrie," Ma replied. "We're almost late as it is. I'm sure you know it perfectly well. I'll hear you say it on the way. Are you ready, Laura?"

"Yes, Ma," Laura said faintly.

Ma blew out the lamp. Outdoors a cold wind was blowing and snow blew white along the ground. Laura's skirts whipped in the wind, her hoops crawled up maddeningly, and she feared that the curl was coming out of her bangs.

Desperately she tried to remember all that she must say, but she could not get beyond, "America was discovered by Christopher Columbus in 1492. Columbus, a native of Genoa in Italy—" Carrie was breathlessly chanting, "'Waiting the hour when at God's command—'"

Pa said, "Hullo, they've got the church lighted up."

Both the schoolhouse and the church were lighted. A thick, dark line of people with splotches of yellow lanternlight was moving toward the church.

"What's up?" Pa asked, and Mr. Bradley answered, "So many have come, they can't all get into the schoolhouse. Owen's moving us into the church."

Mrs. Bradley said, "I hear you're going to give us a real treat tonight, Laura."

Laura hardly knew what she answered. She was thinking, "Christopher Columbus, a native of Genoa in Italy—America was discovered by Christopher Columbus in 1492. Christopher Columbus, a—" She had to get past Columbus.

In the entry the crowd was so jammed that she feared her wire hoops were pressed out of shape. There was no more room for wraps on the hooks there. The aisles were packed with people trying to find seats. Mr. Owen was heard repeating, "These front seats are reserved for the scholars. Pupils please come forward to these seats."

Ma said she would take care of the wraps. She helped Carrie out of her coat and hood while Laura took off her coat and hat and nervously felt her bangs.

"Now, Carrie, you have only to do as well as you have been doing," Ma said as she straightened Carrie's full plaid skirt. "You know your piece perfectly."

"Yes, Ma," Carrie whispered. Laura could not speak. Dumbly she guided Carrie up the aisle. On the way Carrie pressed back against her and looked up pleadingly. "Do I look all right?" she whispered.

Laura looked at Carrie's round, scared eyes. One whisp of fair hair straggled above them. Laura smoothed it back. Then Carrie's hair was perfectly sleek from the middle parting to the two stiff braids hanging down her back.

"There, now you look just right!" Laura said. "Your new plaid dress is beautiful." Her voice did not seem to be hers, it was so serene.

Carrie's face lighted up, and she went wriggling past Mr. Owen to her classmates in the front seat.

Mr. Owen said to Laura, "The pictures of the Presidents are being put up on the wall here, just as they were in the schoolhouse. My pointer is on the pulpit. When you come to George Washington, take up the pointer, and point to each President as you begin to speak about him. That will help you remember the proper order."

"Yes, sir," Laura said, but now she knew that Mr. Owen was worrying, too. She, of all persons, must not fail, because hers was the principal part in the Exhibition.

"Did he tell you about the pointer?" Ida whispered, as Laura sat down beside her. Ida looked like a dim copy of her usual happy self. Laura nodded, and they watched Cap and Ben, who were tacking up the pictures of the Presidents on the board wall, between the studding. The pulpit had been moved back against the wall to leave the platform clear. They could see the long school pointer lying on it.

"I know you can do your part, but I'm scared," Ida quavered.

"You won't be when the time comes," Laura encouraged her. "Why, we are always good in history. It's easier than the mental arithmetic we've got to do."

"I'm glad you have the beginning part, anyway," Ida said. "I couldn't do that, I just *couldn't.*"

Laura had been glad to have that part because it was more interesting. Now there was only a jumble in her head. She kept trying to remember all that history, though she knew it was too late now. But she must remember it. She dared not fail.

"Please come to order," Mr. Owen said. The School Exhibition began.

Nellie Oleson, Mary Power and Minnie, Laura and Ida and Cap and Ben and Arthur filed up onto the platform. Arthur was wearing new shoes, and one of them squeaked. In a row, they all faced the church full of watching eyes. It was all a blur to Laura. Rapidly Mr. Owen began to ask questions.

Laura was not frightened. It did not seem real that she was standing in the dazzle of light, wearing her blue cashmere and reciting geography. It would be shameful to fail to answer, or to make a mistake, before all those people and Pa and Ma, but she was not frightened. It was all like a dream of being half-asleep, and all the time she was thinking, "America was discovered by Christopher Columbus—" She did not make one mistake in geography.

There was applause when that was over. Then came grammar. This was harder because there was no blackboard. It is easy enough to parse every word in a long, complex-compound sentence full of adverbial phrases, when you see the sentence written on slate or blackboard. It is not so easy to keep the whole sentence in mind and not omit a word nor so much as a comma. Still, only Nellie and Arthur made mistakes.

Mental arithmetic was even harder. Laura disliked arithmetic. Her heart beat desperately when her turn came and she was sure she would fail. She stood amazed, hearing her voice going glibly through problems in short division. "Divide 347,264 by 16. Sixteen into 34 goes twice, put down 2 and carry 2; sixteen into 27 goes once, put down 1 and carry 11; sixteen into 112 goes seven times, put down 7 and carry naught; sixteen into 6 does not go, put down naught; sixteen into 64 goes 4 times, put down 4. Three hundred and forty-seven thousand, two hundred and sixty-four divided by sixteen equals—twenty-one thousand, seven hundred and four."

She need not multiply back to make sure the answer was right. She knew it was right because Mr. Owen set another problem.

At last he said, "Class dismissed."

Through a great noise of applause, they all turned and filed back to their seat. Now the younger pupils would speak their pieces. Then Laura's turn would come.

While one after another the girls and boys were

called to the platform and recited, Laura and Ida sat still and stiff with dread. All the history that Laura knew raced madly through her mind. "America was discovered . . . The Congress of Confederated Colonies in Philadelphia assembled . . . 'There is only one word in this petition which I disapprove, and that is the word Congress . . .' Mr. Benjamin Harrison rose and said, 'There is but one word in this paper, Mr. President, which I approve, and that is the word Congress.' . . . 'And George the Third . . . may profit by their example. If this be treason, gentlemen, make the most of it!' . . . Give me liberty or give me death. . . . We hold these truths to be self-evident. . . . Their feet left bloody tracks upon the snow. . . ."

Suddenly Laura heard Mr. Owen say, "Carrie Ingalls."

Carrie's thin face was strained and pale as she made her way to the aisle. All the buttons up the back of her plaid dress were buttoned outside-in. Laura should have thought to button her up; but no, she had left poor little Carrie to do the best she could, alone.

Carrie stood very straight, her hands behind her back and her eyes fixed above the crowd. Her voice was clear and sweet as she recited:

"Chisel in hand stood a sculptor boy
    With his marble block before him,
And his face lit up with a smile of joy
    As an angel dream passed o'er him.

He carved that dream on the yielding stone
With many a sharp incision;
In Heaven's own light the sculptor shone—
He had caught that angel vision.

"Sculptors of life are we as we stand,
With our lives uncarved before us,
Waiting the hour when at God's command
Our life-dream passes o'er us.
Let us carve it then on the yielding stone
With many a sharp incision.
Its Heavenly beauty shall be our own—
Our lives, that angel vision."

She had not once faltered, nor missed a single word.
Laura was proud, and Carrie flushed rosily as she
marched smiling down to her place amid a loud clapping of hands.

Then Mr. Owen said, "Now we will listen to a review of the history of our country from its discovery to
the present time, given by Laura Ingalls and Ida
Wright. You may begin, Laura."

The time had come. Laura stood up. She did not
know how she got to the platform. Somehow she was
there, and her voice began. "America was discovered
by Christopher Columbus in 1492. Christopher
Columbus, a native of Genoa in Italy, had long sought
permission to make a voyage toward the west in order
to discover a new route to India. At that time Spain
was ruled by the united crowns of—"

Her voice was shaking a little. She steadied it and went carefully on. It did not seem real that she was standing there, in her blue cashmere held grandly out by the hoops, with Ma's pearl pin fastening the lace cascade under her chin, and her bangs damp and hot across her forehead.

She told of the Spanish and the French explorers and their settlements, of Raleigh's lost colony, of the English trading companies in Virginia and in Massachusetts, of the Dutch who bought Manhattan Island and settled the Hudson Valley.

At first she spoke into a blur, then she began to see faces. Pa's stood out from all the others. His eyes met hers and they were shining as slowly he nodded his head.

Then she was really launched upon the great history of America. She told of the new vision of freedom and equality in the New World, she told of the old oppressions of Europe and of the war against tyranny and despotism, of the war for the independence of the thirteen new States, and of how the Constitution was written and these thirteen States united. Then, taking up the pointer, she pointed to George Washington.

There was not a sound except her voice as she told about his poor boyhood, his work as a surveyor, his defeat by the French at Fort Duquesne, and then of his long, disheartening years of war. She told of his

291

unanimous election as the First President, the Father of his Country, and of the laws passed by the First Congress and the Second, and the opening of the Northwest Territory. Then, after John Adams, came Jefferson, who wrote the Declaration of Independence, established religious freedom and private property in Virginia, and founded the University of Virginia, and bought for the new country all the land between the Mississippi and California.

Next came Madison, the war of 1812, the invasion, the defeat, the burning of the Capitol and the White House in Washington, the brave sea-battles fought by American sailors on America's few ships, and at last the victory that finally won independence.

Then came Monroe, who dared to tell all the older, stronger nations and their tyrants never again to invade the New World. Andrew Jackson went down from Tennessee and fought the Spanish and took Florida, then the honest United States paid Spain for it. In 1820 came hard times; all the banks failed, all business stopped, all the people were out of work and starving.

Then Laura moved the pointer to the picture of John Quincy Adams. She told of his election. She told of the Mexicans who had fought a war of independence, too, and won it, so that now they could trade where they pleased. So down from the Missouri went the Santa Fe traders, across a thousand miles of desert, to trade with Mexico. Then the first wagon wheels rolled into Kansas.

Laura had finished. The rest was Ida's part.

She laid down the pointer and bowed in the stillness. A loud crash of applause almost made her jump out of her skin. The noise grew louder and louder until she felt as if she must push against it to reach her seat. It did not stop even when at last she reached her place beside Ida and weakly sat down. It went on until Mr. Owen stopped it.

Laura was trembling all over. She wanted to say an encouraging word to Ida, but she could not. She could only sit and rest, and be thankful that the ordeal was past.

Ida did very well. She did not make one mistake. Laura was glad to hear the loud applause for Ida, too.

After Mr. Owen had dismissed the audience, getting out of the church was slow work. Everyone stood between the seats and in the aisles, talking about the Exhibition. Laura could see that Mr. Owen was pleased.

"Well, little Half-Pint, you did a fine job," Pa said when Laura and Carrie had pushed through the crowd to him and Ma. "You did, too, Carrie."

"Yes," said Ma. "I am very proud of you both."

"I did remember every word," Carrie agreed happily. "But, oh, I am glad it's over," she sighed.

"*So—am—I,*" said Laura, struggling into her coat.

Just then she felt a hand on the coat collar, helping her, and she heard a voice say, "Good evening, Mr. Ingalls."

She looked up into the face of Almanzo Wilder.

He did not say anything and neither did she, until they were out of the church and following Pa's lantern along the snowy path. The wind had died down. The air was very cold and still, and there was moonlight on the snow.

Then Almanzo said, "I guess I ought to have asked you if I may see you home."

"Yes," Laura said. "But anyway, you are."

"It was such a tussle, getting out of that crowd," he explained. He was silent a minute and then asked, "May I see you home?"

Laura could not help laughing, and he joined in.

"Yes," Laura said. She wondered again why he was doing this, when he was so much older than she. Mr. Boast, or any friend of Pa's, might see her safely home if Pa was not there to do it, but now Pa was there. She thought he had a pleasant laugh. He seemed to enjoy everything. Probably his brown horses were tied on Main Street, so he was going that way, anyway.

"Are your horses tied on Main Street?" she asked him.

"No," he answered. "I left them on the south side of the church, out of the wind." Then he said, "I am making a cutter."

Something in the way he said it gave Laura a wild hope. She thought how wonderful it would be to go sleighriding behind those swift horses. Of course he could not mean to ask her, still she felt almost dizzy.

"If this snow holds, there ought to be some good

sleighing," he said. "It looks like we're going to get another mild winter."

"Yes, it does, doesn't it?" Laura answered. She was sure now that he would not ask her to go sleighing.

"It takes some little time to build just right," he said, "and then I'm going to paint it, two coats. It won't be ready to take out till some time after Christmas. Do you like to go sleighing?"

Laura felt as if she were smothering.

"I don't know," she replied. "I never went." Then boldly she burst out, "But I'm sure I would like to."

"Well," he said, "I'll come around some time in January and maybe you'd like to go for a little spin and see how you like it. Some Saturday, say? Would that suit you?"

"Yes. Oh, *yes!*" Laura exclaimed. "Thank you."

"All right, then I'll be around, in a couple of weeks if this weather holds," he said. They had come to the door, and he took off his cap and said good night.

Laura fairly danced into the house.

"Oh, Pa! Ma! what do you think! Mr. Wilder's making a cutter, and he's going to take me sleighriding!"

Pa and Ma glanced at each other, and it was a sober glance. Laura quickly said, "If I may go. May I? Please?"

"We will see when the time comes," Ma answered. But Pa's eyes were kind as he looked at Laura and she was sure that when the time came, she could go sleighriding. She thought what fun it must be, to go speeding swiftly and smoothly through the cold, sunny air, behind those horses. And she could not help thinking in delight, "Oh, won't Nellie Oleson be *mad!*"

UNEXPECTED
IN DECEMBER

Next day was blank and limp. They would not try again to have Christmas without Mary. The only presents hidden away were for Carrie and Grace, and though Christmas was not until tomorrow, they had opened that morning the small Christmas box from Mary.

There would be a whole week without school. Laura knew that she should improve the time in study, but she could not settle down to her books.

"It's no fun studying at home when Mary isn't here to study with," she said.

298

Dinner was over and the house all in order, but it seemed empty without Mary in her rocking chair. Laura stood looking around the room as though searching for something she had lost.

Ma laid down her church paper. "I declare I can't get used to her being gone, either," she said. "This piece by a missionary is interesting, but I have read aloud to Mary for so long that I can't properly read to myself."

"I wish she hadn't gone!" Laura burst out, but Ma said she must not feel so.

"She is doing so well in her studies, and it is wonderful that she is learning so many things—running a sewing machine, and playing the organ, and doing such pretty beadwork."

They both looked toward the small vase made of tiny beads, blue and white, strung on fine wire, that Mary had made and sent home for them all for Christmas. It stood on the desk near Laura. She went to it and stood fingering the bead fringe around it as Ma talked on.

"I am a little worried about how we are going to find the money for the new summer clothes she needs, and we must manage to send her a little spending money. She should have a Braille slate of her own, too. They are expensive."

"I'll be sixteen, two months from now," Laura said

hopefully. "Maybe I can get a certificate next summer."

"If you can teach a term next year, we may be able to have Mary come home for a summer vacation," said Ma. "She has been away so long, she ought to come home for a little while, and it would cost only the railroad fare. But we must not count our chickens before they are hatched."

"I'd better be studying, anyway," Laura sighed. She was ashamed of her moping idleness, when Mary had the patience to do such perfect work with tiny beads that she could not see.

Ma took up her paper again and Laura bent over her books, but she could not rouse herself from her listlessness.

From the window, Carrie announced, "Mr. Boast is coming! And there's another man with him. That's him now, at the door!"

"'That is he,'" said Ma.

Laura opened the door and Mr. Boast came in, saying, "How do you do, everyone? This is Mr. Brewster."

Mr. Brewster's boots, his thick jacket and his hands showed that he was a homesteader. He did not have much to say.

"How do you do?" said Ma as she placed chairs for them both. "Mr. Ingalls is over in town somewhere.

How is Mrs. Boast? I am disappointed that she did not come with you."

"I didn't plan to come," said Mr. Boast. "We just stepped in to speak to this young lady," and his black eyes flashed a look at Laura.

She was very much startled. She sat very straight, as Ma had taught her, with her hands folded in her lap and her shoes drawn back beneath her skirts, but her breath caught. She could not think what Mr. Boast meant.

He went on. "Lew Brewster, here, is looking for a teacher for the new school they are starting in their district. He came in to the School Exhibition last night. He figures that Laura's the teacher they want, and I tell him he can't do better."

Laura's heart seemed to leap and fall back, and go on falling.

"I am not old enough yet," she said.

"Now, Laura," Mr. Boast said to her earnestly, "there is no need to tell your age unless someone asks you. The question is, Will you teach this school if the county superintendent gives you a certificate?"

Laura was speechless. She looked at Ma and Ma asked, "Where is the school, Mr. Brewster?"

"Twelve miles south of here," Mr. Brewster replied.

Laura's heart sank even further. So far from home, among strangers, she would have to depend entirely upon herself, with no help at all. She could not come home until the school term was over. Twelve miles and back was too far to travel.

Mr. Brewster went on, "It's a small neighborhood. The country around there isn't settled up yet. We can't afford more than a two-month's school, and all we can pay is twenty dollars a month and board."

"I'm sure that seems a reasonable sum," said Ma.

It would be forty dollars, Laura thought. Forty dollars! She had not realized that she could earn so much money.

"Mr. Ingalls would rely on your advice, I know, Mr. Boast," Ma added.

"Lew Brewster and I knew each other back East," said Mr. Boast. "It's a good chance for Laura if she'll take it."

Laura was so excited she could hardly speak. "Why, yes," she managed to stammer. "I would be glad to teach the school if I could."

"Then we must hurry along," said Mr. Boast as he and Mr. Brewster stood up. "Williams is in town, and if we can catch him before he starts home, he'll come over and give you the examination right now."

They had said good day to Ma and hurried away.

"Oh, Ma!" Laura gasped. "Do you think I can pass?"

"I believe you can, Laura," Ma said. "Do not be excited nor frightened. There is no occasion to be. Just pretend that it is a school examination and you will be all right."

It was only a moment before Carrie exclaimed, "That's him now—"

"'This is he,'" Ma said almost sharply.

"That's he coming— It don't sound right, Ma—"

"'Doesn't sound right,'" said Ma.

"Right straight across from Fuller's Hardware!" cried Carrie.

The knock came at the door. Ma opened it. A large man, with a pleasant face and friendly manner, told her that he was Williams, the county superintendent.

"So you're the young lady that wants a certificate!" he said to Laura. "There's not much need to give you an examination. I heard you last night. You answered all the questions. But I see your slate and pencil on the table, so we might as well go over some of it."

They sat together at the table. Laura worked examples in arithmetic, she spelled, she answered questions in geography. She read Marc Antony's oration on the death of Caesar. She felt quite at home with Mr. Williams while she diagrammed sentences on her slate and rapidly parsed them.

Scaling yonder peak, I saw an eagle
Wheeling near its brow.

"'I' is the personal pronoun, first person singular, here used as the subject of the verb 'saw,' past tense of the transitive verb 'to see.' 'Saw' takes as its object the common generic noun, 'eagle,' modified by the singular article, 'an.'

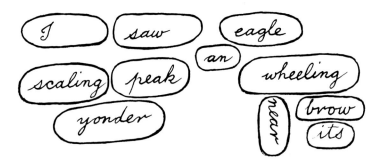

"'Scaling yonder peak' is a participial phrase, adjunct of the pronoun, 'I,' hence adjectival. 'Wheeling' is the present participle of the intransitive verb, 'to wheel,' here used as adjunct to the noun, 'eagle,' hence adjectival. 'Near its brow' is a prepositional phrase, adjunct of the present participle of the verb 'to wheel,' hence adverbial."

After only a few such sentences, Mr. Williams was satisfied. "There is no need to examine you in history," he said. "I heard your review of history last night. I will cut your grades a little for I must not give you more than a third grade certificate until next year. May I have the use of pen and ink?" he asked Ma.

"They are here at the desk," Ma showed him.

He sat at Pa's desk and spread a blank certificate on it. For moments there was no sound but the faint scratch of his sleeve on the paper as he wrote. He wiped the pen-point on the wiper, corked the ink bottle again, and stood up.

"There you are, Miss Ingalls," he said. "Brewster asked me to tell you that the school opens next Monday. He will come for you Saturday or Sunday, depending on the looks of the weather. You know it is twelve miles south of town?"

"Yes, sir. Mr. Brewster said so," Laura replied.

"Well, I wish you good luck," he said cordially.

"Thank you, sir," Laura answered.

When he had said good day to Ma and gone, they read the certificate.

DEPARTMENT OF EDUCATION

DAKOTA   COUNTY OF KINGSBURY

Teacher's Certificate

This is to certify that *Miss Laura Ingalls* Has been examined by me and found competent to give instruction in *Reading, Orthography, Writing, Arithmetic, Geography, English Grammar, and History*

and having exhibited satisfactory testimonials of Good Moral Character, is authorized by this

Third Grade Certificate

to teach those branches in any common school in the country for the term of twelve months.

Dated this *24th* day of *December, 1882*

Geo. A. Williams, Supt. of Schools, Kingsbury county, D.T.

Result of examination:

Reading, 62, Writing, 75, History, 98, English Grammar, 81, Arithmetic, 80, Geography, 85

Laura still stood in the middle of the room, holding that certificate, when Pa came in.

"What is it, Laura?" he asked. "You look as if you expect that paper to bite you."

"Pa," Laura said, "I am a schoolteacher."

"What!" said Pa. "Caroline, what is this?"

"Read it." Laura gave him the certificate and sat down. "And he didn't ask me how old I am."

When Pa had read the certificate and Ma had told him about the school, he said, "I'll be jiggered." He sat down and slowly read the certificate again.

"That's fine," he said. "That's pretty fine for a fifteen-year-old." He meant to speak heartily but his voice had a hollow sound, for now Laura was going away.

She could not think what it would be to teach school twelve miles away from home, alone among strangers. The less she thought of it the better, for she must go, and she must meet whatever happened as it came.

"Now Mary can have everything she needs, and she can come home this next summer," she said. "Oh, Pa, do you think I—I *can* teach school?"

"I do, Laura," said Pa. "I am sure of it."

Laura Ingalls Wilder was born in 1867 in the log cabin described in LITTLE HOUSE IN THE BIG WOODS. As her classic Little House books tell us, she and her family traveled by covered wagon across the Midwest. She and her husband, Almanzo Wilder, made their own covered-wagon trip with their daughter, Rose, to Mansfield, Missouri. There Laura wrote her story in the Little House books, and lived until she was ninety years old. For millions of readers, however, she lives forever as the little pioneer girl in the beloved Little House books.

Garth Williams began his work on the pictures for the Little House books by meeting Laura Ingalls Wilder at her home in Missouri, and then traveling to the sites of all the different little houses. His classic illustrations caused Laura to remark that she "and her folks live again in those pictures." Garth Williams also created the illustrations for CHARLOTTE'S WEB, STUART LITTLE, and almost one hundred other books.